The Reinvention of Chastity

Eve Vaughn

A Samhain Publishing, Ltd. publication.

Samhain Publishing, Ltd.
512 Forest Lake Drive
Warner Robins, GA 31093
www.samhainpublishing.com

The Reinvention of Chastity
Copyright © 2007 by Eve Vaughn
Print ISBN: 1-59998-426-1
Digital ISBN: 1-59998-379-6

Editing by Angie James
Cover by Scott Carpenter

First Samhain Publishing, Ltd. electronic publication: February 2007
First Samhain Publishing, Ltd. print publication: December 2007

Dedication

To my friends who keep me motivated, the hussy brigade, sexual chocolate and the freaky bunch. Thanks for the love and the laughter.

Chapter One

"It's no big deal; I'll have Chastity do it for me. She's always willing to help out. Not once has she complained when I've given her extra work to do. I'd have to say she's one our most valued employees." Sebastian's voice filtered from his slightly cracked office door.

Upon hearing her name, Chastity halted. At that moment she realized turning around would probably be best, but something kept her rooted to the spot. She'd been told once that an eavesdropper never heard anything good about themselves, but what could be the harm in listening this one time? Besides, what she'd just heard wasn't bad at all. She *didn't* mind the extra work given to her from time to time.

Normally she arrived at the office before anyone else, so it had surprised her to see her boss's car in the parking lot before eight o' clock. Sebastian rarely put in an appearance before nine. Chastity had intended to leave him an iced coffee in his mini-refrigerator as she usually did on Monday mornings, and a fresh, homemade blueberry muffin on his desk. He never asked for it. It was just one of the many things she liked doing for him.

Eve Vaughn

"I think you expect an awful lot of her. She's only one person you know. I think you'd be up shit's creek if she decided to leave the firm." That voice belonged to Jeremy Owens, the other partner in the Rossi & Owens law firm.

"In the event of that happening, I'll hire someone else. I fail to see the problem."

"The problem is that you put too much work her way and depend on her far more than you should."

"Chastity has never let me down before, besides all I have to do is drop a couple of hints and she'll drop everything on her desk to help out."

"You're so wrong."

"What's so wrong about it? She gets paid for her time. Hell, she probably makes nearly as much as the two of us with all the overtime she puts in—well not as much as us, but you get the picture."

"It's still not right how you work her so hard."

"The choice is hers, not mine. Her work is not unappreciated, and I thank her at every opportunity. She's not forced to stay late, and out of the two years she's been with the firm I can count on one hand the number of times I've actually had to *ask* her to work overtime."

"You're playing coy with me, Seb. You know as well as I do why she really busts her ass for you," Jeremy lightly scolded.

"So, she has crush on me. It's nothing serious, I'm sure."

"And you have no problem using it to your advantage?"

"Why shouldn't I? It's a cutthroat world out there, and I haven't done anything to lead her on."

"She's a very nice lady who doesn't deserve to be used like that. You'd better be careful, my friend, because one day you're going to get a taste of your own medicine."

"Well, it's not like she has much of a life anyway." Sebastian's deep, throaty laughter filled his office.

"How would you know?"

"Do you see any pictures of loved ones on her desk? Does she ever talk about anything other than her cats? Hell, I bet the woman hasn't been laid in years, if ever." There was a brief pause and then a curse from Sebastian. "I wonder where she is. She usually has an iced coffee waiting in the fridge for me on Mondays."

Chastity felt the walls closing in on her. A sensation of being kicked in the stomach shot through her, making it nearly impossible to breathe. Much worse, how could Sebastian talk about her in such an offhand manner? The way he told it, she was just a sexless, emotionless drone to be called upon to handle his every whim. Maybe she didn't have a wild whirlwind of social activities lined up, but it had never been something she'd obsessed over.

Up until now it hadn't bothered her. Chastity knew she should walk away but instead stepped closer to the door to listen better. Some kind of self-destructive impulse kept her neck craned closely toward the sound of the two lawyers' voices. "It's really none of my business, but since you bring the subject up, her lack of a social life doesn't justify using her for your own selfish means," Jeremy argued.

"When have I ever made any of our employees do anything they didn't want?"

"I'm not saying you do, but it certainly doesn't stop you from exploiting her crush on you. I mean, all you have to do is crook your little finger and that woman rushes to do your bidding like you're the greatest thing since sliced bread. It's really a shame she doesn't know what a true bastard you can be when it comes to women."

"I don't need this shit so early in the morning. Like I said, I've never encouraged her crush. She's a nice lady, but not exactly my type. I like my women a little more polished. Anyway, I can hardly be blamed for her schoolgirl infatuation."

"No, it's not your fault, but at least stop acting as if you don't know exactly what you're doing. Just when I think your ego can't get any bigger, you always manage to surprise me." A brief silence followed before Jeremy spoke again. "I'll be in court for most of the day. I only came by to get some papers. See you tomorrow."

Chastity backed away from the door as Jeremy's voice grew closer.

"Wait, man," Sebastian halted his friend. "Are we still on for a game of hoops tomorrow night?"

She didn't wait around to hear Jeremy's response. By the time he stepped out of Sebastian's office, Chastity was already around the corner, racing to the bathroom, tears running down her cheeks. Charging through the restroom door, she realized she still held the muffin and iced coffee, which she promptly threw in the garbage can.

How pathetic would it have looked for her to take Sebastian breakfast when he obviously thought so little of her? Sinking down onto the closest toilet seat and shutting the stall, she let her head drop into trembling hands. Sobs racked her body, misery freely flowing.

In just one moment, Sebastian Rossi had stripped her of every bit of dignity she possessed without even realizing it. Perhaps what he'd said wouldn't have been so bad if it weren't so goddamn true. No, she didn't have much of a social life. Yes, her cats were probably the most exciting things in her life, but did it warrant such censure? The other cutting thing was learning that he knew of her feelings for him. He'd ripped a hole in her soul, and then laughed.

Chastity couldn't figure out what was worse out of the two. How could she face him now? The only solution that came to mind was to look for another job, anything so as not to see him again. She'd been working for Rossi & Owens for two years and from the moment she'd set eyes on Sebastian Rossi, her entire world came to a screeching halt. Whenever he drew near, her body would tighten. Her nipples would grow stiff as she'd imagine his large tanned hands cupping the undersides of her breasts. Everything about him made her body seize up with lust—from the smell of his cologne, to the devilish twinkle in his pale green eyes.

Whenever Chastity took notes for him, she sometimes found herself staring at the sensual curve of his cranberry lips. Even the way he walked, with slow, fluid movements, made her pant. She couldn't count the hours she'd spent fantasizing about his tall, lean and taut body. Oddly, Sebastian wouldn't be considered handsome by most. Striking most certainly, but not handsome. His face had too much character for such a weak term, with its tad too long nose and thick black brows slashing angrily over eyes that made him look slightly sinister. His craggy features were all hard planes and harsh lines, but when Sebastian Rossi walked into a room, women took notice.

He carried with him a larger-than-life presence that had helped him rise to one of Philadelphia's top personal injury attorneys. Intelligence and sharp wit only magnified his appeal. There was no doubt about it; he was the epitome of sex on two legs.

And she was just another dummy who fell for him.

Of course he wouldn't want someone like her. She was short and borderline chubby. At best, she was cute. At worst,

Eve Vaughn

she was a bit on the plain side. Chastity shuddered when she thought of all the times she'd stayed late because Sebastian granted her one of those devastating smiles of his.

Biting her bottom lip, she recalled how she'd drop everything she was working on just to do his bidding. On top of it all she went above and beyond what any paralegal did at the firm, like bringing him breakfast and volunteering to run errands for him even though he had a secretary.

"How pathetic," she muttered. To know she'd been taken advantage of sucked. In the back of her mind, she'd always known she wasn't Sebastian's type, because he seemed to favor the tall, willowy model type. At least with him, she knew race wasn't a factor, so she couldn't use her being black as a reason he wasn't interested in her. Brunettes, blondes, redheads, black, white and Asian: Chastity had seen quite a few of his girlfriends when they visited the office, but none remotely resembled her. Instead, every single one of them looked liked they'd stepped off the cover of a high fashion magazine.

She removed her glasses to wipe her tears away before slipping them back on her face. A brief glace at her watch told her it was time to begin work. Grabbing some toilet paper to blow her nose, she left the bathroom stall. Chastity walked to the mirror to make sure she looked presentable. No, she'd never be a bombshell, but she had nice skin, a smooth, rich dark cocoa, and full, curvy lips. She'd been told her smile was nice, to which she agreed, especially when a deep set of dimples popped out.

Her large, dark brown eyes weren't bad either, heavily lashed and tilted slightly up; they had the disadvantage of being covered by huge, thick, horn-rimmed glasses. She'd already reconciled with the fact that she'd never win any beauty pageants. Hadn't her mother always told her not to shoot beyond her reach?

10

Patting her hair, which she kept pulled back into a tight bun, she frowned noticing an inch of new growth. It was time for a touch up at the beauty salon. Chastity took a deep breath and made her way out of the restroom. An impending sense of doom flowed through her when she made it back to her desk.

The moment she sat down to work, her nasty co-worker, who sat at the desk a few feet away from her, started in on Chastity. "Well, if it isn't little Miss Punctuality. I was surprised you weren't already typing away like the good little employee you want everyone to believe you are," the older woman sneered.

If she hadn't been taught to respect her elders, Chastity would have told Pearl off a long time ago. She had to be one of the most unpleasant people to be around. "If you don't mind, I'd rather not talk. I have a lot on my mind," she answered with a sigh.

"Well excuse me, miss. I'm just trying to make conversation."

"And I'm just trying to work, Pearl. I have a lot to get through today," Chastity said as patiently as she could.

"Are you implying that I don't have a lot of work to do?" Pearl took offense so easily; it was hard to say something without the woman getting her back up.

"I said no such thing."

"You certainly implied it."

Chastity silently counted to ten. "I apologize if that's how it sounded, but it wasn't what I meant."

"Hmph," was the only reply from the grumpy woman.

Great, now Pearl would be on her case all morning. This day was going from bad to worse.

ଈଔଈଔ

"Girl, you know I love you, but you can't sit around whining about it. You have to take action," Dallas Jamison said, flipping a stray lock of black hair from her eyes.

"Come on, Dallas, can't you see the kid is miserable? The least we can do is offer her some support," Kevin chimed in.

Dallas pursed her lips. "Support my ass. What the hell do you think we've been doing for the past couple hours? I've been here since six o' clock and it's now eleven. Right now I could be getting laid and having a couple cocktails, not necessarily in that order. And what about you, Kevin? You should be spending time with Nick but nooo, we're both here for Chastity's pity party. The time for crying is over, my friend."

Chastity's head shot up as she glared at her best friend since middle school. Dallas was gorgeous to look at with her even mahogany skin and slanted chocolate eyes that gave her a cat-like appearance. Her triangular shaped face was framed with a neat glossy black chin-length bob. Tall and lithe, she looked exactly like the type Sebastian would go for, which made Chastity feel even more miserable.

Dallas was probably right. What was the point in crying about it? The damage was done, but damn, the humiliation still burned strong. "What would you have me do? I mean, it'll probably take a while for me to find another job as high paying as the one I have now. You have no idea how it felt this morning walking into the office just to hear Sebastian rip me apart like I'm the biggest loser of the century." Her fingers tightened over her Calico cat Monty's neck, causing him to hiss furiously. "I'm sorry baby," she murmured, setting the angry feline free.

"You see? Even Monty doesn't want to be around right now, and who knows what happened to Fluffy," Dallas pointed out, untangling long legs from under her before standing up, arms akimbo.

Chastity recognized that determined gleam in her friend's eyes and knew a plan was hatching. Uh-oh. The last time Dallas had that particular look, Chastity ended up with a broken leg. "Save me, Kevin," she whispered to the blond sitting at her side.

Kevin shrugged, probably realizing that he could no more stop Dallas than she could. "This should be interesting," he muttered, raking long fingers through short, spiky hair.

"I don't think you should quit your job," Dallas mused. "I think you should seduce him and then when you have him where you want him, dump his ass. Show him how little his feelings mean to you. I guarantee it'll teach that bastard not to walk all over you again. Who the hell does he think he is anyway, to treat you like that?"

"Are you on crack? If you haven't realized, I'm not exactly seduction material, and there's a little issue about my short, pudgy body. I think he prefers his women with a little less meat on their bones."

Dallas rolled her eyes. "You're nowhere near fat, not even pleasantly plump. You're thick and do you know how many men love thick women? Look at Oprah, Queen Latifah and Tocara from that modeling show. There's more cushin' to the pushin', baby."

"Said the size six," Chastity snorted.

"Actually, I'm a size four, thank you very much. Don't let the big booty fool you." Dallas winked, rubbing well-manicured hands over her hips.

Flipping her friend the bird, Chastity shook her head. "Bitch."

The other woman grinned, blowing her a kiss. "But you love me anyway."

"Unfortunately," Chastity sighed. Even though Dallas's idea was completely preposterous, she giggled at the thought of seducing Sebastian. Something like that would never happen.

Kevin's dark eyes narrowed, giving Chastity a discerning look. "You know, I think the idea has merit. Nick could take you shopping. He loves getting his hands on a new project. It'll be just like *Pretty Woman.*"

"I don't want to be anyone's project."

"I think that's a great idea, Kevin." Dallas jumped from one foot to the other in excitement as though Chastity hadn't said a word. "I'll take her to the salon to get her hair styled. She has a fine grade of hair. I wish she didn't wear it pulled back into that tired-looking bun all the time. She'll definitely need to get those brows shaped, along with a manicure and pedicure. We'll hook her up!"

Kevin nodded, beaming from ear to ear, revealing big white teeth. "It's a must that we get rid of those coke bottle glasses. I've always thought they were hideous. They make her eyes look like tiny raisins."

That was it. Chastity couldn't just sit like a lump while they dissected her as if she were some specimen on a Petri dish. Raising her hand, she said, "Uh, hello? I'm sitting right here and I think I'm just fine the way I am. I realize I could lose a few pounds, but I don't need your makeover help." She couldn't believe their audacity. Sure Dallas shot straight from the hip, but Chastity was surprised at her neighbor and good friend of three years, Kevin. Considering his job was that of a corporate sensitivity trainer, Chastity expected a little more support.

"I hate to tell you, hon, but your style does leave little to be desired. Nick and I were just talking about it the other day. Just because you're not a Tyra or Naomi, doesn't mean you can't be sexy. Let's face facts, nearly all of your skirts practically touch the floor and those blazers make you look like my nana," Kevin went on ruthlessly.

Chastity crossed her arms over ample breasts. "Well, sorry if my sense of fashion offends you. We don't all have the luxury of being born a gay man."

"Stop playing the martyr. It's time for you to take charge of your life. Make him notice you, and then squash him like the rat he is." Kevin emphasized the point by slamming his fist in his palm.

"Even if I do get a makeover, it won't necessarily mean he'll suddenly want me."

Dallas sighed. "Maybe not, but at least you can show him that you don't give a damn about what Sebastian Rossi thinks. Besides, if our plan doesn't work out exactly as we want it to, you just may find someone more worthy of your devotion. When was the last time you got laid anyway?"

"Is nothing sacred with you, Dallas?"

Her friend shrugged impatiently. "Just answer the question."

Chastity shook her head in disbelief, unable to believe the turn this conversation had taken. "That's none of your business."

"Don't be such a prude, girl. If you can't tell your friends, who can you tell?" Dallas asked, plopping back down on the loveseat with her usual dramatic flair.

Kevin took Chastity's hand in his, giving her a wink. With his blond hair, guileless brown eyes and wholesome face, he had the All-American-boy-next-door looks that made women drool. Why were the cute ones either assholes or gay? "Enquiring minds want to know, honey," he drawled.

Chastity sighed. There was no point in trying to keep anything from these two. "It's been about four years, but I will have you know that I choose to be celibate."

A look of horror crossed Dallas's face. "Are you saying the last guy you slept with was Melvin Sloane? Eww. He looked like Urkel's twin brother, but not as cute."

"Oh stop that. He wasn't that bad and you know it. Melvin was a nice guy and he wasn't a bad lover either."

Her girlfriend laughed. "As if you have a lot to compare him to."

"Three partners is nothing to sneeze at. Unlike you, I prefer being in a relationship before I'm intimate with a man. I don't do random penises."

"And where has that gotten you?" Dallas shot back. "You spend your nights alone curled up on the couch. You get up and go to work, then come home. I have to practically beg you to hang out with us sometimes. That's not living, girl."

Chastity's face burned with embarrassment. She didn't see anything wrong with being careful about choosing sex partners, but when put like that, her life sounded as exciting as cold dishwater.

Sebastian's deep laugher filled her mind. *It's not my fault she has a crush on me.* Thinking of all the hours she'd put in to help around the office while the rest of the staff had gone home, raised her ire. Then she remembered the times she'd showered him with compliments. There was even a time when she'd brought him homemade cookies.

And he laughed behind her back.

Who the hell did he think he was to trample over her feelings, unknowingly or not? What gave him the right to think she was someone to tread upon—someone he could treat like a wind-up-doll, just because he could? Apparently he thought he had every right to do so, and she only had herself to blame.

Well no more Miss Nice Guy. For the first time that day she was angry. No, she was pissed. Maybe she'd never be the femme fatale Dallas and Kevin wanted to make her into, but Chastity swore to herself that she'd bring Sebastian Rossi to his knees if it was the last thing she did.

"Okay, guys. You win. When do we start? I'm ready to be reinvented."

Chapter Two

Something fishy was going on.

Sebastian checked his watch, and then his desk clock to make sure the times matched. What the hell had gotten into Chastity? Out of the seven paralegals at the firm, she was generally the most dependable. If he needed a subpoena drafted or a letter written, Sebastian knew he could count on her. He never had to ask her to stay late. It was just something she volunteered to do, arriving early and leaving late.

Beyond her cats, she never talked about anyone special in her life, so it never occurred to him that she had much of a life. He was well aware of her crush on him. He'd be an idiot not to notice, especially by the way she stared at him, her eagerness to please and the constant chatter.

At first, Sebastian found her attention a little embarrassing and contemplated letting her go, but since she didn't act upon those feelings, he was able to ignore them. Now he was just used to it. He freely admitted there were times when he'd use those feelings to his advantage. Guilt would assail him, but he managed to push it away, convincing himself that she enjoyed doing his bidding, so why knock a good thing?

Chastity was a nice lady and a damn good worker, but she just wasn't his type. She reminded him of his twelfth grade math teacher, round and frumpy. He supposed she could be attractive if she did a little more with her appearance and got rid of those thick glasses. Where the hell did she find those things anyway? They looked like something straight out of the fifties.

He had to admit though, that smile of hers was rather arresting. It was actually kind of pleasant coming to the office to see a bright smile greeting him in the morning. And despite the many layers of clothes she favored wearing, they didn't disguise a very generous rack. Once, he'd even wondered what she'd look like stripped beneath his gaze. Would she be a hellcat in bed? The quiet ones usually were. Not that it really mattered anyway. He preferred his women taller and...more pleasing to the eye.

As superficial as that may be to some people, why should he settle for someone who obviously didn't take pride in her appearance? Sure she was neat and clean, but that wasn't enough for him. Perhaps he was the hopeless snob, where women were concerned, his mother accused him of being, but it was how he felt.

Sebastian glanced at his watch again and frowned. It was now nine-thirty. Chastity had left a message with the receptionist, saying she'd be running late. She should have been in the office an hour ago. Normally, he didn't really have time to notice when his employees were tardy, unless the office manager brought it to his attention, but it wasn't like Chastity to be late at all.

In fact, all last week, her behavior had been odd. Whenever Sebastian would ask her to do something for him, she'd hesitate, not attacking the task with her usual eagerness. When he spoke to her, she didn't meet his eyes. Not even a smile tilted her lips when he walked by. There almost seemed to be an air of resentment surrounding her.

Had he done something to her? Said something offensive? Sebastian racked his brain, trying to figure out the reason for the total about-face. It shouldn't have bothered him so much, especially if it meant her being over him, but it did. It bothered the hell out of him.

He'd even asked Chastity about her stupid cats, just to get a smile out of her, but the only reply had been a curt, "fine". What did it matter? She was just an employee anyway. As long as she did her job, that should be that.

Just then his office door burst open. His partner Jeremy stepped inside and closed the door behind him, a flushed look on his face. Sebastian knew that look well. Jeremy had big news.

"Aren't you supposed to be in court this morning?"

"No. It's been postponed. Dugan filed a motion to dismiss. Judge Larson won't have a decision until the end of the week," the blond answered, flopping down into the chair in front of Sebastian's large oak desk.

"Does he have a leg to stand on?"

"Not really. He's probably just trying to buy more time. The case is cut and dry. His clients clearly ignored the safety regulations, which caused Mr. Jones' injury. I'm not sure why they haven't discussed a settlement yet. I have a feeling Dugan's trying to dig up some dirt on my guy."

"Dugan is such an ass. He probably told his clients they could win. I bet he's trying to drag this out for as long as he can to pad his wallet. I'm just surprised he hasn't been brought before the ethics committee yet."

Jeremy nodded in agreement. "I hear you. It's attorneys like him who give the rest of us a bad name."

Nothing disgusted Sebastian more than a crooked attorney. There were lots of slimy lawyer jokes and Irwin Dugan epitomized most of them. It had been a shady lawyer who was indirectly responsible for Sebastian's chosen profession. His parents were both second generation Italian-American, both raised to believe in the American dream.

Franco and Marina Rossi instilled in their children the value of hard work and family. Though they'd not been wealthy in terms of money, in love and unity they lacked for nothing. There was no one Sebastian had loved more than his father and no one he wanted to be like more.

Franco encouraged his son's dream of becoming a professional basketball player. At fifteen, Sebastian had been the star of his high school basketball team. His dream came to a screeching halt however, when he'd come home one day to find his mother in hysterics. He'd never forget that day as long as he lived.

"What's wrong, Mama? What's going on?" he'd asked. Before she could respond, Sebastian instinctively knew something had happened to his father. It was just the type of connection he and his father had.

It turned out that Franco had been fatally injured on the job while working with faulty machinery. To add insult to injury, the company he'd work at for nearly twenty years, refused to pay the death benefit. At the urging of family, Marina consulted an attorney who not only promised to get them what the family was owed, but much more. When all was said and done, the charlatan's fee was greater than the piddling amount the company grudgingly paid in the end, leaving the family in debt.

Sebastian wrote several letters to the Bar Association, to no avail. To make matters worse, with his father's death there was no health insurance, which was devastating because Marina had three children to support, including a daughter with special needs. It had been a humbling experience for all of them to live off of their relatives' charity. What the lawyer had done left a lasting impression on Sebastian.

It gave him an interest in the law. Winning a basketball scholarship at Temple University, he chose pre-law as his major. After graduating summa cum laude he was accepted into law school at the University of Pennsylvania where he decided to specialize in personal injury law.

Not long after passing the bar on his first try, Sebastian soon secured a position in one of Philadelphia's top firms, where he made a name for himself. It was also where he met Jeremy. He worked at that particular firm for five years, when he and his friend decided to start their own law firm. His success enabled him to move his mother into her own home, equipped things that would make life easier for his sister as well. Sebastian also helped his brother through medical school.

Because of what happened to his family, Sebastian took on several pro bono cases and he never led his clients on. If he felt there was a case he fought hard for them, but if he thought there wasn't, he said so. He prided himself on his stellar reputation in the law community and no amount of money was worth selling out his integrity.

"Earth to Sebastian." Jeremy leaned over the large desk waving a hand in Sebastian's face, breaking him out of silent musings.

"Huh?"

"Where were you, man?"

"Oh, I was just thinking."

"What about?"

"It isn't important. What's up with you bursting into my office like a lunatic?"

Jeremy's lips twisted sardonically. "I didn't think I needed to make an appointment to see you."

"Of course you don't. So, what's got you all excited?"

"You'd know if you saw Chastity walk into the building this morning."

Sebastian frowned. What the hell was his friend talking about? He couldn't think of a single thing that would cause excitement about his frumpy paralegal. "Chastity Bryant? What about her?"

"She doesn't look like the same person. It's like the extreme makeover team got their hands on her. I swear, I didn't recognize her when she walked by me."

Jeremy wasn't prone to exaggeration, but Sebastian had a hard time picturing Chastity with any type of makeover. "It's about time she decided to do something with herself, but how different can she look?"

"Sebastian, she's hot."

"Now I know you're pulling my leg, especially when I know the type of bimbos you date."

"Yeah, like you're one to talk. You get more ass than a toilet seat."

Sebastian shrugged. "I've worked hard to get where I am today. There's nothing wrong with dating around, as long as I'm safe."

Jeremy wiggled dark blond brows at him. "It's a little more than dating, don't you think?"

"Go to hell."

"We're going together, remember? Anyway, as I was saying, you have to check her out."

"Uh, maybe later. I just can't picture Chastity looking any better than she usually does," Sebastian sighed. The very thought was laughable.

"Okay, but remember, I saw her first."

In the middle of taking a sip from his coffee mug, Sebastian spit out the hot liquid at his partner's words. "Are you kidding me?" he asked, grabbing some napkins from inside his desk and started to blot up the mess he'd made.

"I'm as serious as a heart attack."

"What happened to that reporter you were dating? I thought things were getting pretty hot and heavy with the two of you."

"Justine? She dropped the M-bomb so you know what that means."

"Perhaps if you were more upfront with your women in the beginning of the relationship, you wouldn't go through this over and over again."

Jeremy chuckled with his usual air of nonchalance. "We can't all be Casanova, with women throwing themselves at us like we're super studs."

"Cut it out. You have no room to talk, pretty boy."

Rolling his eyes heavenward, Jeremy shook his head. "I wish you wouldn't call me that. Anyway, I just thought I'd stop by with the office buzz."

"Really? The entire office is talking about her transformation?"

"I'm telling you, it's dramatic."

"Okay, I'll walk by her desk later, but I have to get through these briefs, so I'll talk to you later."

Jeremy stood up. "Sure. Just to let you know, I have a ten o' clock consultation, so I'll be indisposed for the rest of the morning."

"Okay." Sebastian waved his friend out of his office before turning his attention back to the paperwork on his desk. Alone again, yet he couldn't concentrate. Damn Jeremy, for making him think about someone he normally didn't give much thought to beyond the work she produced for him.

"How different can she be?" he muttered.

Sebastian tried his best to focus on the work before him, but after several failed attempts, he gave up. "Shit." He stood and walked out of his office. Curiosity had gotten the better of him. When he made it to Chastity's desk, she wasn't there.

"Hiya, boss," Pearl Addison, another paralegal, greeted him with a brief salute before turning back to her computer.

"Good morning, Pearl. Um, have you seen Chastity?"

"She said something about getting some files. I guess she'll be back in a few minutes. I'll tell her that you came by." The woman gave him a small smile that didn't quite reach her eyes. Pearl looked old enough to be his grandmother. She was an efficient worker and that was all that mattered to him. He sometimes got the distinct impression that she didn't really approve of him for some reason.

"If she won't be long, I think I'll wait for her. Did you have a good weekend?"

Pearl looked slightly annoyed by the question, but answered pleasantly enough. "My weekend was just fine, thank you. Me and the hubby went to visit my daughter in New York. Poor Carl grumbled the entire way there about the price of gas, but what can you do?"

"Yes, the prices are getting out of hand, aren't they?"

Faded blue eyes narrowed slightly. "I'm sure you're really feeling it with that big Escalade you drive." Her voice dripped with scorn.

"Yes. I've been driving my other car lately."

"Oh...the Mercedes?" she spat the words out with borderline contempt. Sebastian would be damned if he apologized for his wealth and didn't feel the need to explain to Pearl how he supported his family and gave to charity on a regular basis. He worked very hard to be in the position he was in now and to have someone look at him as though he didn't have the right to spend his money as he pleased, annoyed him.

"Yes, I've been driving the Mercedes lately. With all the nice spring weather we've had lately, I've been able to drive with the top down," he answered with a smile. *Take that old lady.*

Pearl's lips pressed together in a tight line of disapproval, but she wisely said nothing. He hadn't realized how unpleasant she was. Jeremy had been the one to hire her.

"Mr. Rossi, is there something I can help you with?" a familiar feminine voice asked from behind him.

Sebastian whirled around and nearly fell backwards at the sight that greeted him. His eyes widened in surprise. No. It couldn't be. Could it? Chastity raised one perfectly arched eyebrow, obviously waiting for his response. "Chastity?"

Her full, glossy, plum-colored lips curved into a smile. "If you don't mind, could you move out of the way so I can put these files down? They're getting kind of heavy."

He couldn't move to save his life, even when he realized what an idiot he must have looked. She rolled her eyes and sidestepped him, then dropped the files on her desk. Sebastian looked her up and down, taking in every single detail, yet still not believing what he saw.

Jeremy had been wrong. She wasn't hot—she was breathtaking. He found himself temporarily robbed of speech. Gone were the thick, unattractive glasses, revealing large, thickly lashed dark eyes. Why had he never noticed her sensually curved lips before? Or the small mole resting at the top corner, emphasizing their sexiness? They looked like they'd been made for kissing. He had the sudden urge to capture those skillfully painted lips with his until she begged for air.

Her smooth, dark brown skin glowed with health, barely hinting at the use of make-up, which he was sure she was wearing. Sebastian found it difficult to look away. Chastity's normally pulled-back hair was now fashioned around her face in a riot of soft curls that cascaded to her shoulders. When his gaze slid over her outfit, his balls tightened and his cock stirred.

Small, round women had never been his cup of tea, but seeing the generous amount of cleavage displayed by her low-cut beige top made it difficult to tear his eyes away. She shifted her weight from one leg to the other, and it was apparent that she was growing impatient, but he couldn't help it. The transformation was nothing short of miraculous.

Damn, she had nice legs too! Short women weren't supposed to have well-shaped, curvy legs like that. She had the cutest dimpled knees he'd ever seen. He liked what he saw. A lot. Sebastian's mouth watered. His tongue snaked out to dampen his now dry lips as he imagined wrapping his arms around the ample armful in front of him and—wait a minute. What in the world was he thinking?

This was Chastity Bryant for God's sake, his employee. Even if he couldn't tear his eyes away from her, she wasn't his type. Right? Chastity was the one to finally break the silence, an indiscernible expression in her dark eyes. "If you don't need me for anything, I have a lot of work to do," she said, turning her back to him, her round bottom taunting him.

27

Sebastian's hands covered the front of his pants when his cock grew uncomfortably hard. What the hell? Only minutes ago, he couldn't give a flying fuck about her, but now he was standing in the middle of his firm, rock hard and dying to pull that juicy backside against him. If he made any sudden movements, he'd draw attention to his...problem. Not to mention, he was extremely annoyed at being dismissed so offhandedly.

His pride was stung. Who was this body snatcher and where was she hiding the pod with the real Chastity? First, the strange behavior of last week and now the stunning transformation from caterpillar to butterfly, what was next?

"Oh, actually there are a few things I'd like to go over with you, but it will be lengthy. Maybe we can discuss it over lunch." The minute the words were out of his mouth, he regretted them. He'd never once invited her for lunch for work or otherwise, so where did that come from?

Her eyes widened with apparent surprise. "I'm sorry Mr. Rossi, but I have plans for lunch. Is it possible to have this meeting later in the day?"

Was she kidding? If he weren't so damn horny right now he'd point out that she worked for him and not the other way around. "Fine," he said through gritted teeth. "Come to my office in half an hour with notepad and pen." Sebastian turned around abruptly and strode off before he further embarrassed himself.

He wasted no time getting back into his office and closing the door firmly behind him. Once seated, he unzipped his pants and eased his cock out. He curled his fingers around the base of his throbbing erection and slid them along his hard length. Sighing in relief, he couldn't believe he was masturbating in his office like some untamed schoolboy. How was it possible that a woman, who he wouldn't have given a second thought to before this metamorphosis, could bring him to this point? And so suddenly?

God, he ached.

No woman had ever made him feel this sexual pull so instantly. Sebastian squeezed his eyes tight as he remembered the tangy scent of her perfume and how he'd wanted to bury his face against her delectable chocolate neck. He imagined what she'd look like naked under his gaze, her large breasts overflowing in his hands. Would she have large nipples? Would they be dark like blackberries and how would they taste.

The images were driving him insane and he didn't like it one bit. This was madness. He gripped his cock more firmly, stroking it with frenzied motions. Biting his lip to suppress a moan, he felt his balls tightened. Sebastian quickly grabbed a tissue from his desk to catch his ejaculate as he reached a satisfying orgasm.

Once his breathing was under control, and tissue discarded, he glanced at his watch. Now that he had gotten that out of his system, he'd be able to act normally when Chastity came to his office, despite her glamorous appearance.

It had been a while since he'd gotten laid. That could be the only explanation for his reaction. Yes. That had to be it. His last relationship had ended over two months ago. All he'd have to do was look through his little black book and the problem would be solved. Or would it? He certainly hoped so, because lusting after Chastity was not a good idea.

Chapter Three

A slow smile tugged at the corner of her lips. Chastity hadn't known what Sebastian's reaction would be to her new look, but she hadn't expected to see the unhidden look of lust in the depth of his light green eyes. She may not have much experience with the opposite sex, but it was impossible to mistake that raw hunger. In a way, it had excited her to see the appreciative look on his face, but on the other hand, it scared her.

No one had ever looked at her like that before. Of course there'd been boyfriends, but they'd been staid and boring. If the truth were told, Chastity's past relationships lacked fire. She instinctively knew it would be different with Sebastian. There was no doubt in her mind that he'd leave her satisfied and panting for more. She could easily find herself falling for him all over again, so she'd have to tread lightly.

It had taken every ounce of willpower within her not to go doe-eyed on him. Only reminding herself of the humiliating things he'd said about her strengthened her resolve to remain passive. Dallas would be so proud of the cool-as-a-cucumber attitude Chastity displayed when confronted by Sebastian.

She could hardly believe she looked like this herself. Having grown up in a single-parent home, raised by a young mother who felt the need to compete with her daughter whenever a boy was brought home, shattered her self-esteem. Chastity supposed it was the reason she'd never done much with her appearance before. She'd just given up when she realized that she could never outshine her gorgeous mother, who never seemed to let her forget it.

The fear of being found lacking carried over into adulthood. It was something she should have gotten over by now at thirty-one years old, but old scars were difficult to heal. Perhaps the Sebastian incident had been just what she needed to turn her life around. Just as her friends had promised, they'd taken her in hand. Kevin, along with his boyfriend Nick, an artist with a killer fashion sense, had raided her closet and thrown nearly all of her wardrobe in the trash.

Then they took her to South Street where they commenced putting a huge dent into her savings, picking out clothes, shoes and accessories. They found tasteful clothing that not only showed off her voluptuous figure to its advantage, but concealed her trouble spots as well.

Nick and Kevin showed her the kind of outfits that would flatter her and what wouldn't so she could shop on her own in the future. No longer could she use her size as an excuse to dress like someone's grandma. It had been an exhausting excursion.

The next day Dallas snapped Chastity's glasses in two, forcing her to wear the contacts Chastity never touched. Then they headed to a spa where she was treated to a deep tissue massage, a pedicure, manicure and makeover. The make-up artist taught her how to apply the make-up as artfully as she had. After the spa, the two women took a trip to the hairdresser where Chastity received a fresh relaxer and trim. Her hair had been styled into soft curls. The result with the hair, make-up and clothing was more than she expected. For the first time in her life, she felt beautiful.

There was no feeling in the world like walking down the street and turning heads. It was truly an empowering experience and she loved it. *Now remember, you have to be ice cold to Sebastian. Bring him to his knees, girlfriend.* Dallas's words drifted through her consciousness. Chastity glanced at her silver wristwatch, seeing that she needed to be in Sebastian's office in five minutes.

She silently congratulated herself once again on how she'd handled herself with him.

"Aren't you a cool one this morning, Miss Pig—I mean Chastity?" Pearl's harsh voice sliced through her thoughts. The Miss Piggy comments were getting tiresome. Complaints to the office manager did no good, because Pearl would claim she'd been heard incorrectly, all while smiling sweetly.

It didn't matter, because Chastity wasn't going to allow the old bat get under her skin.

When Chastity didn't respond, Pearl continued to needle. "I see you're ignoring me. Do you think you're hot stuff now that you've finally done something with yourself?"

"Not at all, Pearl. I have a lot on my mind right now, is all."

"Humph. I know what's on your mind and just because you got yourself a makeover, it doesn't mean the boss is finally going to notice you."

Last week this comment would have gotten under her skin, but Chastity simply smiled. That's exactly what she was banking on, but she wanted Sebastian to do more than just notice her. Still, she didn't respond to the annoying woman who seemed to grow more agitated with each passing second.

"I was talking to you, missy," Pearl hissed.

On the verge of telling Pearl to shut the hell up, she bit her lip. No, she wouldn't let this woman ruin her day. "I know you were, Pearl, but I'm not sure how I'm supposed to respond to that statement."

The other woman snorted. "Well, I hope you don't start acting all high and mighty just because you look halfway decent now. You still need to lose weight," she finished nastily.

Chastity's smile widened and she looked Pearl straight into her faded blue eyes. "I appreciate your concern, but I promise I won't start acting that way, especially since you have the market cornered on high and mighty around here. Now that I've tried something new, why don't you do something new as well, like minding your own business?"

Pearl's face turned beet red to the roots of her silver hair. "Well, I never! That's what's wrong with the world today. You young people don't know the meaning of the word respect."

"You have to give respect to in order to get it. You've been nasty to me since I started working here and frankly, I'm tired of it. I'm not going to allow you to use your age as an excuse, so now if you'll excuse me, I have a meeting with Mr. Rossi." Chastity stood, pad and pen in hand, and turned her back on the gaping woman.

Screw her.

As Chastity walked away, she heard Pearl mutter under her breath. She didn't care what the cantankerous woman was saying. That heffa could kiss her big black ass. As she passed the receptionist's desk she gave a little wave.

"Chastity, is that you?" Debbie's large blue eyes widened.

"Yes, what do you think?" She twirled around with a flourish.

Debbie looked at her with faintly envious eyes. "You look fabulous. I knew you could be a stunner if you put your mind to it. I've been hearing about this new look around the office all morning. Whatever you did to yourself, you have to let me in on your secret."

"It's no secret. I just got rid of the granny gear and let my hair down. Anyway, you don't need to do a thing for yourself, you look great."

"You're a sweetie—hold on." Debbie answered the ringing phone.

"I'll catch you later," Chastity whispered, looking down at her watch again. Shoot. Five minutes late. She knew Sebastian's pet peeve was tardiness. She walked to his office to find the door open and a sudden nervousness hit her. As though sensing her presence, Sebastian's head lifted from the papers he'd been intently studying.

His eyes narrowed, shooting blue fire. "What took you so long?" he barked.

Chastity took a step back, her courage slowly slipping away. Stay strong, she told herself. Squaring her shoulders, she stepped inside the office. Why did he have to look so good?

"How about closing the door behind you?"

"Excuse me?" Had she heard him correctly? Sebastian had never asked her to close the door to his office before.

"I said close the door. Did your new look damage your hearing?"

His rudeness caught her off guard, making her gasp.

He sighed. "That was uncalled for, Chastity. I apologize. Would you please close the door?"

"Why?"

"So that we can have some privacy, I need to go over this case with you."

"As long as we've worked together, you never asked for privacy before," she pointed out.

An irritated look crossed his chiseled face as he shot out of his chair with a curse. "For the love of God, it was a simple request, woman." Storming over to the door, he closed it with a decisive click. Sebastian glared at her before sitting back down. "Now, do you think we can get started without you questioning my every request?"

Chastity couldn't hold back her smile. Day one and she was already getting under his skin. Sebastian didn't seem like he could take his eyes off her.

He raised one dark, thick brow. "What are you grinning about?"

"You're being really cranky this morning. Hard night?"

"I don't know what's gotten into you, but I'm not sure I like it," he muttered. "And what the heck happened to you anyway?"

"A little of this and that. I thought you said you wanted to discuss work?" Chastity smiled at him again, crossing and uncrossing her legs in a deliberate play for his attention. She didn't miss the way his eyes followed the motion. Chastity cleared her throat when he didn't speak.

"Huh? Oh, yeah." He tugged at his tie as if it were chocking him.

She raised the notepad over her mouth to hide yet another smile. "Chastity, if you're finished playing hide and seek, let's get down to business," he said gruffly.

They began to discuss one of his upcoming cases. It was for one of his pro bono clients. Chastity had worked for other law firms and none of them gave back to the community as much as Sebastian did. It was one of the reasons she'd always admired him. He genuinely seemed to care about the people he represented and took his job seriously. For a man with such an excellent work ethic, it was a shame that he was such a rat where women were concerned.

They became so deeply engrossed with their discussion that the interruption of his telephone was jarring. "Hold on a second," he said before answering. "Sebastian Rossi speaking." A large smile split his face after a brief pause. "Robin, this is a pleasant surprise. You could never be a bother, sweet pea."

Who the hell was Robin? Chastity stood, thinking it would be best to give him some privacy. "I'll be back when you're finished."

Sebastian held up his hand to halt her. "I would love to, honey. I appreciate your asking me. Now that we live in the same city I see you even less than before. It should be the other way around."

Chastity felt uncomfortable listening to him talk to whoever this Robin person was. It was obvious he felt a genuine affection for this woman on the other end of the line, and it bothered the hell out of her. It shouldn't have, but it did. She was supposed to be over him, exacting her plan of revenge, but here she was sitting in his office, seething with envy over this mystery woman. Chastity imagined she'd be a gorgeous blonde, or a fiery redhead with big boobs.

"I'm sure whatever you wear will look great." He laughed that deep, throaty, wonderful laugh of his. "I look forward to it, sweet pea. I'll see you then. Love you." He waited for a brief moment before hanging up. "I'm sorry, where were we?" Sebastian seemed to be in a much better mood, but it put Chastity out of sorts. Whoever this mysterious Robin was, it sounded serious.

There was nothing she hated more than a cheater and if Sebastian was currently in a serious relationship, then this would put a wrench in her plans.

"Girlfriend?" She could have punched herself for asking that question. "Sorry. It's none of my business."

Her curiosity seemed to amuse him, his eyes twinkling. "It was my kid sister, why?"

A wave of relief so great swept through her, that she literally slumped in her chair before righting herself. "Just making conversation." Hurriedly she glanced at her notes. "Uh, we were talking about contributory liability and how much of it was the client's fault."

"Are you okay?" he asked.

"What? Oh, I'm fine."

"You were frowning."

Chastity shrugged. "I was just thinking."

"About what? Your little lunch date?" The derisive note in his voice made her sit up taller and pay attention.

"No, actually I wasn't, not that it's any of your business."

"Ah, so it's okay for you to quiz me, but I'm not allowed the same privilege?"

Her face grew warm. He had a point, but she wasn't about to let him turn this thing back on her. "I shouldn't have asked."

"You said you were just making conversation. So let's talk."

"But you didn't call me in here to make conversation. You called me to your office to work, not talk."

A smile touched his sexy lips. "Yes, so I did. I'm sorry, but I have to ask. Why the sudden transformation? I hardly recognize you."

"I don't see what my appearance has to do with anything," she said, not wanting to veer down this road.

"At the risk of starting an argument, I think it does. Along with this new look has come a new attitude and I'm not sure I like it very much."

Because I'm not fawning all over you, she wanted to ask. "The look or the attitude?"

"The attitude I can definitely do without. The look..." His gaze slowly slid over her curves as if he had x-ray vision. "I like very much."

Chastity squirmed in her seat. Had someone turned up the heat in the building? He wasn't supposed to have this affect on her still. Damn the man. "Good for you, but really, as long as I'm getting my work done, what does my attitude matter?"

"Oh, I think it matters a great deal. What happened to the sweet woman who always had a smile on her face? By the way, I haven't seen those adorable dimples of yours in over a week."

Adorable dimples? It surprised her that he'd noticed anything about her before this makeover. She wasn't about to let him charm her back to the doormat she used to be. "I didn't realize smiling was a requirement around here."

"No, it's not, but it's nice to see."

Chastity gave him her biggest smile. "Better?"

"Something tells me you didn't mean it."

"You wanted me to smile. You didn't say that I had to be sincere."

Sebastian threw his head back and laughed. "Perhaps you're the one who should have the law degree. You'd kill them in court. Okay, you win. It occurs to me that as long as you've been working here, I don't know much about you."

A couple weeks ago, Chastity would have loved it if he'd taken an interest in her life, but now his motives were too obvious. "I live alone with my cats Monty and Fluffy. I do believe I've told you about them before. Monty is the spawn of Satan and Fluffy is scared of her own shadow. I spend day and night tending to their needs. They're all that matters in my life," she said, deadpan.

Sebastian's lips twisted. "Stop being so damn facetious. I just asked a simple question."

She shrugged. "Who's being facetious? Isn't it general knowledge that the only thing going on in my life is my cats? You seem to think so, at least." She squeezed her eyes shut. Damn. She'd said too much. Chastity didn't want to reveal her hand so soon.

His brows furrowed together. "What are you talking about? Where would you get that idea?"

She should have known he'd pick up on that little slip. He wasn't one of the city's top lawyers for nothing. "I don't know what you're talking about."

"You can't just make a comment like that and then expect me to let it go."

"Well, you'll just have to," she shot back.

Sebastian stood and walked from behind his desk. Had she pushed him too far? Would he fire her on the spot? He stalked over to where she sat. Chastity gulped, her body once again reacting to his nearness. Her pussy tingled, and panties grew damp. She'd never been more aware of him than she was now, with him standing before her so tall and blatantly male. "Care to say that to my face?" he asked, leaning over her chair.

"Mr. Rossi, you're being ridiculous."

"Don't give me that Mr. Rossi crap. You know we don't run a very formal office and you've always managed to call me Sebastian before." He knelt next to her and gasped her chin between strong fingers. It was the first time he'd ever touched her—deliberately. His pale green eyes flickered with an emotion she'd only seen in her dreams. Desire.

Her heart pounded erratically, so hard she was sure he could hear it. "Chastity, something has been bothering you lately and whatever it is, I wish you'd tell me."

"It's nothing. Absolutely nothing." More than anything she wanted to close her eyes and lean into him, finally feel the touch of his lips on hers, but this was too soon. Too fast. Chastity pulled away from his grasp, her eyes fixing on his wall clock. "Umm, I have to go. It's past twelve and my lunch date is waiting for me."

Sebastian stood abruptly, his eyes going stormy. "Who are you having lunch with? I wasn't aware that you had a boyfriend."

"Why should you know? You're my boss," she answered, trying to play it cool, even though her body screamed for the feel of his arms wrapped around her.

"Fine. Go to your lunch date, but this conversation is far from over."

"Unless it's work related, we have nothing to talk about."

"Oh, I think we do."

"You know what? You have a lot of nerve. First you treat me like a robot, but now that I've changed my look, you're suddenly interested in what's going on in my life. Well, I'd thank you to mind your own business." When she stood to leave, Sebastian's hand snaked out to grab her wrist.

"I'm making you my business, Chastity."

She shivered at the sheer strength in his hold. Judging from the feral gleam in his eyes, she had him right where she wanted him.

Let the fun begin.

Chapter Four

"I'm sorry I'm late, Kev, but my brainstorming session with Sebastian ran a little late." Chastity sat at the table Kevin had saved for them in the quaint Market Street Bistro. Kevin surveyed her from head to toe before approval entered his eyes.

"I'm proud of you, honey. You've kept the look up quite nicely."

Chastity giggled, picking up her menu. "It's only been a couple days, but I plan on keeping it."

"There's something totally different about you, and I'm not talking about the look. You seem more confident and it shows. I think that's one of the reasons why this transformation suits you. I mean, anyone can get a makeover and look presentable, but you make it work. I always knew you could be beautiful, but looking at you now, you're making me consider switching teams."

Laughing out loud, she wagged her finger at him. "Stop that. We both know you're crazy about Nick."

"You're right. He's my soulmate." Kevin sighed, getting that same moony look in his eyes whenever he talked about his partner.

"So, are you two still planning to go to Hawaii and tie the knot next year?"

"That's still up for debate. Nick wants the whole nine yards, with the white picket fence and kids. I'm not sure if I'm ready to take that step. I mean, I love him, but bringing children into this union is a step I've never really considered."

She patted his arm in a supportive gesture. "Well, I'm sure you and Nick will work something out. You two are too perfect together to let this issue come between you." And they were. Chastity was sometimes envious of the close bond her next door neighbors had.

She'd been friends with the two of them since the day she moved into her Cape Cod, just outside of the city in Montgomery County. Other than Dallas, she couldn't ask for two better friends.

A wistful look crossed Kevin's face. "I'm sure it will, but enough about me, how about you? Has Sebastian declared his undying love for you yet? Does he want you to be his 'baby's mama'?"

Chastity snorted. "Hardly."

"You two would make beautiful chocolate and vanilla babies."

She laughed, browsing through the menu. "You're getting way ahead of yourself. First of all, I have no plans whatsoever of having children with Sebastian and secondly, just because he likes the way I look now, doesn't mean it will lead to anything."

"Aha! So he did like the new you. I want details, Chas. What was his exact reaction?"

Chastity proceeded to relay the morning's incident, not leaving out any details. His eyes widened. "Shut up! He asked you out to lunch?"

"He said it was business."

"Well, I knew you'd get a reaction from him, but I didn't think it would be this fast. Wow. I'm impressed."

"And I'm annoyed." She rested her hand under her chin.

"Why?"

Chastity was about to answer when their waiter came to the table to take their order. When they were alone again, Kevin raised a blond brow, obviously waiting for an answer. "Why are you annoyed?"

"It bothers me that even though I've changed on the outside, I'm still the same person on the inside. What was wrong with me before?"

"I can name a few things, hon. Let's face it, Chas, you hid yourself in oversized clothing, wore no make-up and to be honest, I can't really think of a diplomatic way to describe how those glasses made you look. If you didn't care about your appearance before, then why should he? A man likes to see a woman make some effort, you know."

"But he's still a superficial bastard."

"Maybe so, but you can't lay all the blame at his feet, even if he is a weasel. Life isn't always like the movies, where the handsome billionaire notices the plain-Jane girl next door for what she's truly worth."

Chastity scrunched up her face. Why did he have to be so right? Maybe some of it was her fault, but that didn't give Sebastian the right to use her feelings to his advantage. That's what irked her the most. She sighed. "You're right. I guess I let my mother affect me even after putting several hundred miles between us."

"I thought your mother was quite charming, the one time she came for a visit," he said, taking a sip of his coffee.

"My mother is an extremely charming woman...to the opposite sex, of course. I think I would have been better off if I'd been born a boy. That way, she wouldn't have felt the need to constantly compete with me." For as long as Chastity could remember, her mother had always put an emphasis on looks and weight.

Brenda Bryant was blessed with a genetic make-up that enabled her to eat whatever she wanted without gaining a single pound. Chastity had not been so fortunate, taking after her stocky father, who'd passed away before she was born. It was around the time she began developing breasts and boys started noticing her, when Brenda seemed to realize her own mortality.

Whenever Chastity brought a male friend home, her mother would prance around their house in the skimpiest outfits and flirt shamelessly. That wouldn't have been so bad if Brenda wouldn't have pointed out Chastity's flaws in front of her friends. Mentioning the embarrassment to her mother did no good because it was only brushed off with a laugh. "Oh, Chassy, you know I don't mean anything by it. What's the matter, baby? Scared that your mama's going to outshine you?"

Chastity realized her mother would never change and stopped bringing boyfriends around. By the time she'd turned eighteen, she knew she'd never be a great beauty like her mother was, or at least that's what her mother had pointed out to her on so many occasions. "Too bad you don't take after my side of the family." "You don't have good hair like I do." "You're not wearing that, are you?" were comments she'd heard throughout her childhood.

During her freshman year in college, Chastity broke her own rule and brought home a guy she'd had a crush on from the moment she'd laid eyes on him. D'Angelo Green, with his tall, lean body and skin as dark as onyx, made her drool whenever he stepped into a room. He was one of the sexiest

44

men she'd ever met. The problem was, her mother thought so too.

Finding the two of them locked in each other's arms had been the final straw. Her mother, as usual, laughed it off. "I can't help myself sometimes. You know how it is, Chastity. Besides, if you did more with yourself, your little boyfriends wouldn't stray."

D'Angelo had later confessed, "You're cute, but your mom...well you know how it is." Actually, she did know how it was and after that, she stopped caring. Even after finishing college and moving to the Philadelphia area with Dallas, Chastity had a hard time getting over what her mother had done. It affected her to the point where she wanted to make herself as plain as possible. That way, it was okay if someone found her lacking.

She loved her mother, as much as she could. With several hundred miles between them it was easier, but Chastity knew she'd never have the typical mother-daughter relationship with Brenda, who was still chasing her youth.

"Sweetie, you can't keep beating yourself over the head about it. It's time for you to start living in the present," Kevin reasoned.

She released a deep breath, glancing at her watch. "I know, but it's easier said than done. I guess, in a way, I have Sebastian to thank. If not for him, I'd still look like a beauty school reject. He's the one who made me realize how pathetic I actually was. Speaking of Sebastian, I don't have much more time for lunch. I walked here, but I didn't realize how much time it would take on foot."

"No worries, I'll drive you back. Do you think the big bad boss will object because you're a few minutes late? It just might give your Italian Stallion something to think about."

Chastity gave this some thought. "That would be something, wouldn't it?"

"Most definitely."

₨₨₨

Sebastian couldn't take one more second in his office. Where the hell was Chastity? Late to work, and late back from lunch. What was her damn problem? He'd gone by her desk to see if she'd be able to go over a few things with him, but she was still out to lunch, when she should have been back by now. Who was she with and why had she been so secretive? These thoughts were driving him nuts.

He had to get out of the office, if for nothing else than to get some air. Yes. That's what he'd do. A walk down the block would clear his head, and once he got back, he'd be able to put things into perspective. Once outside, far from getting the peace of mind he'd hoped for, he saw Chastity getting out of a sporty, red convertible driven by a blond hulk. What the hell?

Was this new man the reason for her about-face? From the way they smiled at each other, it was obvious the two of them were close. It shouldn't have bothered him to see her with another man, but it did. In less than a day, Chastity had managed to get under his skin, and he didn't like it one bit.

As though his feet had a mind of their own, Sebastian found himself marching toward Chastity as her blond friend drove away with a jaunty wave. "You're late!" he stormed, when he stood less than a foot away from her.

Chastity looked up, eyes widening. Her mouth formed an "O" as if she were trying to get words out but they wouldn't come. Why did her perfume make him delirious with lust and why did he feel the urge to pull her against him? This was unacceptable.

"Well, are you just going to stand there staring at me or do you have an answer to my question?"

Large eyes narrowed. "You didn't ask me a question. You said, 'I'm late', so what could I possibly say in my defense?" The calm tone in which she spoke to him made Sebastian realize what a fool he was making of himself, but that only served to fuel his ire.

"Well, don't just stand there with that stupid expression on your face. The least you could do, is explain why you're late."

"Have I ever been late before?"

"What the hell has that got to do with anything?"

"I think it has a lot to do with it."

"You were certainly late this morning as well. I hope this doesn't become a habit."

"I called in this morning."

"It didn't make you any less late."

Her nostrils flared. "For as long as I've been with this firm, have I ever been late before today?"

"No, but that's beside the point. Tardiness is inexcusable under any circumstances."

"Okay. I'll keep that in mind. I've been duly reprimanded and it won't happen again. Now, if you'll excuse me, I have a lot of work on my desk to take care of." She moved to sidestep him, but his hand reached out, stopping her. Chastity pointedly looked at the hand on her arm and Sebastian instantly let go. With one last look, she swept off, the sway of her hips would have enticed a blind man. Damn. What had just gotten into him?

He'd never railed at any of his employees like that, even if it had been deserved. Chastity certainly hadn't. Sure she'd been late, but she had a point. It wasn't her habit to be tardy. There were a few people in the office who were perpetual offenders, and they had never bothered him half as much as seeing Chastity coming back from lunch with that mystery guy. Jealousy. It was an ugly emotion that made even the most reasonable of men crazy.

Sebastian would be damned if he let her drive him insane. Screw that. The only feasible solution was to get some pussy, and soon, otherwise he was in trouble.

ಸುಜ್ಞಾ

"Sounds like our plan is working better than I thought it would," Dallas said over the phone later that night.

"Yeah, it's kind of weird though. Before, it was like I was a nonentity to him, but now that I have this new look, he has this sudden interest in my life. I'm not really sure how to handle it all."

"Wasn't that the entire point of this whole experiment?"

"Yes, but I'm bothered that I had to change how I looked before he noticed me. Kevin made a good point about guys wanting a woman who took pride in their appearance, but I don't think I was absolutely repulsive before. I only wished he would have noticed me before all of this. The more that I think about it, the more I'm down with the plan."

"While his thinking is a little shallow, girl, even you have to admit that you looked a hot mess. I know you don't want to hear this, but I have to agree with Kevin. And don't give me that song and dance about your mother. We both know the kind of woman she is, but you can't keep letting what she did to you ruin your life."

"I realize that. Anyway, I can't really put all the blame on Mom anymore. Actually, I feel kind of sorry for her."

"Why is that?"

"Think about it. She's always had her looks to rely on, and though I'm sure she'll be one of those women who'll be beautiful until the day she dies, her youth is important to her. It's something she'll never get back, but she continuously pursues all those younger men. And the fact that she can't be without a man, tells me that deep down she never worked on her inside enough to enjoy her own company."

Dallas sighed on the other end of the line. "I'm glad you've finally realized that. Looks are nice to have, but if your self-worth is dependent on having a man, then that's kind of sad. On the flipside, there's nothing wrong with looking nice, as long as you don't go overboard about it."

Chastity giggled. "Well, I've been an ugly duckling for so long, I think I'm going to have fun being the swan from now on."

"Yeah, just don't let it go to your head, or I'm going to kick your ass." Leave it to Dallas to pull no punches.

"I'll keep that in mind," Chastity answered wryly.

"So, what are you going to do about Sebastian?"

"To be honest, I was a bit wary in the beginning about the whole scheme, but just by the way he acted today, I think I can pull this off. Not only that, I'm going to enjoy playing the seductress."

"That's the spirit, girlfriend. You teach him not to toy with your feelings again. If I were you, I'd wait until he proposes marriage and then tell him off."

"Now I know you've lost your mind. I never said anything about marriage, and besides, I don't think he's the marrying type."

"I think you can get him to that point, if you play your cards right. Men like a challenge. Just think about it, you could get him so flustered that he goes down on one knee and proposes to you like a lovesick puppy."

Chastity rolled her eyes. "That's probably not going to happen. The man gets a lot of action, so I'll settle for a little infatuation for now."

"Well," Dallas sounded slightly disappointed, "my plan would devastate him more."

"You're diabolical."

"Thanks! I appreciate the compliment," Dallas laughed.

As they continued to talk, Chastity couldn't help but wonder if she could walk away if Sebastian proposed to her.

Chapter Five

It was official.

Sebastian wanted Chastity Bryant. He'd reached his boiling point and could no longer deny what had begun from the moment she stepped into his office with her glamorous new look two months ago.

It grew more difficult with each passing day to watch her stroll around the office looking drop-dead gorgeous. It wasn't just her looks either. Chastity now exuded a confidence that hadn't been there before, and he found it sexy as hell. He couldn't get a proper night's sleep from thoughts of her. He'd wake up in the middle of the night, body drenched with sweat after dreaming about burying himself between silky, chocolate thighs.

Whenever she walked past him, he couldn't tear his eyes away from her slow, rhythmic movements that seemed to scream, "jump me". He'd already lost count of how many times his dick got hard with just the mere mention of her name. Sebastian wanted to run his hands over her body just to see if that rich, dark skin of hers was as soft as it looked.

Once, he'd caught her nibbling on her bottom lip and he literally had to stop himself from grabbing her and tasting it for himself. Sebastian would sit at his desk for hours trying to concentrate on his work when all he could think about was stripping Chastity's clothes off, one article at a time—tasting every delectable inch of her.

Tossing his pen aside, he stood up in frustration. It was already past twelve. He might as well grab something to eat since he wasn't getting any work done. On his way out of the office he knew he'd pass by Chastity's desk.

His plan to keep walking without looking her way went down the tubes when he spied Jeremy leaning over her desk. Chastity gave his friend the big smile she used to give him. Her eyes twinkled with apparent amusement at whatever Jeremy was saying. The deep dimples in her cheeks gave her a look of sweet innocence.

Since her makeover, Chastity had taken to wearing low cut tops and today was no exception. The sexy décolletage on display was enough to set his pulse racing. His fingers itched to trace the tops of those generous mounds. She wore her hair pulled back into a ponytail tied with a pink satin ribbon. Although he preferred her hair flowing around her shoulders, she looked lovely.

An irrational burst of envy soared through his body, making him clench his fists. Unable to help himself, he walked over to them. "What are you two grinning about over here?" Sebastian cursed inwardly. He didn't mean for his voice to sound so harsh.

They looked up at him, Jeremy eyeing him with mild curiosity and Chastity looking slightly resentful, as though he'd intruded on a private conversation. Jeremy straightened up, an easy smile splitting his face. "What's up, Seb?"

"I was on my way to lunch actually."

The blond frowned. "I thought you had a business lunch with one of your clients."

"They had to reschedule," he lied. He wasn't about to admit that he canceled his appointment because his head was in his pants. "You didn't answer my question."

Jeremy frowned. "What question?"

Sebastian hated repeating himself, especially over something as trivial as this. "What were you two grinning about?"

"Just small talk. Chastity and I were on our way to lunch as well."

Sebastian's blood thundered. He wanted to knock Jeremy on his ass. He remembered his friend telling him of his interest in Chastity, but that didn't stop the green-eyed monster from rearing its head. A demon must have possessed him because he couldn't help saying, "Since we're all headed for lunch, let's all go together." His eyes never left Chastity's face.

Her lips tightened slightly before she turned her head away. She didn't seem pleased.

Tough.

"We were only going to the Gallery Mall, nothing fancy," Jeremy said, almost as if to put him off.

"I don't need anything fancy. You don't mind my tagging along, do you?" Sebastian knew very well that he was putting them in a position where they couldn't refuse without looking like a couple of jerks. The look on Jeremy's face spoke volumes. Chastity's face, however, was unreadable and he wondered what was going on in that beautiful head of hers. "Do you mind, Chastity?"

She looked up at Jeremy with a smile, not bothering to answer Sebastian's question. "I'm going to the restroom before we go."

Jeremy smiled back. "No problem. Take your time."

Both men watched her retreating figure, her curvaceous bottom swaying from side to side with each step she took. God, he wanted her. When she was out of earshot, Jeremy turned on him, blue eyes blazing. "What the hell was that about?"

"What do you mean? I thought you said you didn't mind my joining you two."

"You know damn well I couldn't say otherwise."

"Why couldn't you? I would have."

"Don't play dumb with me, Romeo."

Sebastian shrugged. "Who's playing dumb? Haven't we had lunch together on numerous occasions?"

"Not with Chastity."

"Okay, fine. What's wrong with a little friendly competition?"

For a second, it looked like Jeremy wanted to deck him before his face relaxed into a smile. "You're a son of a bitch."

Sebastian laughed. "And don't you forget it."

"She's going to see right through this new interest you have in her. You never gave two flying fucks about her before this sudden change."

"Neither did you."

"Okay, so we're both bastards."

Sebastian cocked an eyebrow and held out his hand. "May the better bastard win?" Even as they shook hands, Sebastian guaranteed himself the victory.

The three of them decided to have a meal at a small tavern not too far from the office instead of trekking all the way downtown to the Gallery Mall. When shown to a booth, Jeremy slid in next to Chastity and Sebastian took the seat directly across from her. That was fine with him. This way, he could face her, and she'd have no choice but to look at him as well.

He wouldn't allow her to ignore him, if he had any say in the matter.

The look of agitation on her pretty face told him that he was getting to her as well. Good. He wanted her to be as aware of him as he was of her.

"I think the Cobb salad looks good. Have you eaten here before, Jeremy?" she asked, turning to the blond. Sebastian knew exactly what Chastity was up to, but if she wanted to play games, she'd soon learn just how competitive he could be.

Fixing his gaze on his prey, he said, "Chastity, why don't you try the Oysters Casino. A nice little aphrodisiac, don't you think?"

She only spared him a brief glance before her eyes darted away again. She fluttered thick lashes at Jeremy as if he were some kind of rock star. "I'm not really in the mood for anything heavy. What do you think, Jeremy?"

"Hmm, I think I'll have a hamburger and fries. Probably not the healthiest choice, but I'll just have to hit the gym a little harder tonight."

"I think I'm going to stick to the salad. My ass is big enough as it is." She closed the menu with a sigh.

Jeremy grinned at her wolfishly. "At the risk of sounding like a lecher, I think your ass is just fine."

Chastity giggled, dimples popping out. Before Sebastian realized what was going on, his lunch mates fell into a deep conversation, completely excluding him. His fury grew with each passing second. By the time the waitress took their orders, he was ready to strangle them both. He knew what Jeremy was up to, but what was up with Chastity's cold shoulder act? No woman had ever treated him like this before and it was driving him bananas. He hated being ignored, especially when it was by someone he wanted so damn much.

It was time to step the game up a notch. "Chastity," he said her name softly, but loud enough for her to hear. She turned her head, a frown marring her pretty face.

"What?"

"Did I tell you how lovely you look today?"

The expression on her face told him that his comment came as a surprise. "Thank you," she murmured, her eyes sliding away from his.

"You've looked lovely every day this week. Pink is definitely your color. You should wear it more often. I like the way it looks against your skin." Chastity squirmed in her seat. Sebastian smiled. "What's the matter, Chastity?"

She kept her lids lowered, not replying.

Jeremy answered for her. "Isn't it obvious? You're embarrassing her."

Sebastian smirked. "Is that true? Am I embarrassing you? I thought all pretty women enjoyed receiving compliments."

Dark eyes lifted, shooting daggers in his direction. "The compliments I don't mind but..." Her voice trailed off before she tightened her lush lips.

Sebastian placed his hands on the table, leaning forward. The smell of her perfume wafted to his nostrils, tickling his senses with its flowery fragrance. "But, what, Chastity?"

"I just rather you didn't."

The blaring shrill of a cell phone ring cut through the air. It was for Jeremy. "Jeremy Owens, speaking." He listened for a moment, then covered the mouthpiece and lowered it. "Excuse me. I'm going to have to take this." Sliding out of the booth, he gave them an apologetic look.

Chastity looked like she wanted to toss something at Sebastian when they were alone. A chuckle erupted from his throat. "Alone at last, my pretty," he purred.

"Why?" came her clipped demand.

"Why what?"

"Why did you invite yourself to lunch with us? How did you know Jeremy and I didn't have something to discuss...privately?"

He didn't like the way she'd emphasized that last word. Was she now switching her attention to his partner? Over his dead body would he allow that to happen. "Why are you willing to have lunch with Jeremy and not with me?"

"Because I like Jeremy."

She couldn't have made a more hurtful statement. Trying hard not to wince, Sebastian looked her straight in the eye, the smirk returning to his face. "Well, let's get to know each other better, and I'm sure you'll find something to like."

"I've learned all I want to know about you in the past two years and I'm not impressed." Chastity picked up her glass of diet soda, sliding the straw between crimson colored lips. His cock jumped to attention while he watched the slim white tube disappear a centimeter at a time into her mouth, before she took a sip. Her eyes locked with his as the steady stream of fluid flowed down her throat. Never in his life had he been jealous of an inanimate object. He wanted to be that straw in the worse way.

She was doing it on purpose. He was sure of it. When she lifted her head she ran her tantalizingly pink tongue over full lips. Pushing the drink away from her, Chastity sighed. "You know what?"

"What?" he croaked. His throat had gone dry.

"You're an arrogant son of a bitch. The Earth doesn't revolve around you."

"Now wait just a—"

"No. You wait a minute. Don't think I don't know what you're trying to pull."

"Just what game do you think I'm playing?"

With a slight twitch of her lips and a rise of her brow, she looked him up and down. "You want me."

Sebastian's jaw dropped. He'd originally thought Chastity had been abducted by pod people, and now he was sure of it. Pod person or not, she was absolutely right. He wanted her like crazy. "But I suppose you're going to tell me that you don't want me."

"On the contrary, I want you too."

He didn't know whether to be relieved or skeptical at that statement. "You could have fooled the hell out of me. So, why the ice princess act? You've been giving me attitude for the past two months."

She shrugged one pink-clad shoulder. "That's not important."

"I think it is. And what about Jeremy? The two of you seemed pretty chummy earlier."

"You sound jealous." Her dimples appeared when she bared small white teeth. Chastity's smile lit up her entire face. Sebastian found it enchanting even though she was driving him nuts. Why had he never noticed these little subtleties before now? "Maybe I am."

"There's no need to be. Jeremy is a nice guy, but I have a thing for tall Italian men with eyes the color of freshly grown grass."

He smiled at her detailed description. "It sounds like you've spent a lot of time thinking about my eyes."

"So?" She grinned unrepentantly, before taking another sip of her soft drink. Whatever had brought on this about-face, Sebastian had no plans to delve into the reasons why. He couldn't afford to, because his cock told him to take advantage of the moment.

"You have beautiful eyes too. Why you used to wear those horrible glasses is beyond me."

The very same eyes he'd just complimented narrowed slightly, and he knew he'd said the wrong thing, but the smile returned to her face. "Yes, they were horrible weren't they?" she agreed.

"Chastity, I'm not going to beat around the bush—"

"Then don't."

"Fair enough. I want to take you out."

Her face remained impassive. "Sounds boring."

"I beg your pardon?" Why the hell was he working so hard for this woman who displayed Sybil-like tendencies?

"There's no pardon to beg. Look, I'm going to make this easy for you. The only reason you want to take me out is to get into my pants. You'll wine and dine me, tell me the things you think I want to hear, and say how enchanting I look or how beautiful my skin is. Or something equally as corny, but when it all comes right down to it, you're hoping to get me into the sack."

"Well I—"

She held up her hand. "No explanation needed. Like I said, I'm going to make this easy for you. You want to fuck me, and I'm going to let you. I don't need dinner or flowers. Just you."

Was this a wet dream? Was Chastity really sitting here in front of him saying that all she wanted was to fuck? He was on the verge of answering when Jeremy chose that moment to reappear.

"Sorry about that, guys. I had a call from the office."

Son of a bitch!

Just when things were getting interesting between him and Chastity, his friend had to show up and ruin everything. Chastity winked at Sebastian before turning her attention back to Jeremy. Throughout the remainder of lunch, Sebastian barely touched his food. Watching her eat with slow deliberate bites was a sensuous experience. And when she ate one of Jeremy's fries, slipping the golden potato wedge into her mouth, he broke out in a sweat.

Sebastian knew she was doing it on purpose, with the sly glances under her long lashes and the way she leaned forward just a little too much, revealing the tops of her big chocolate breasts. The waitress came back.

"Would you guys like dessert?" She smiled down at him. She was a cute redhead with an athletic physique, but he only spared her a moment's glance.

Chastity turned to the waitress, a mischievous grin tilting her lips. "Do you serve cherry pie?"

"No, ma'am, but we do have a very good apple pie."

Chastity pouted. "Oh, that's too bad. Well never mind." She then turned to Sebastian. "There's plenty of time for cherry pie later."

The double entendre wasn't lost on him. His control had finally reached its limits. He had to get up or else explode right then and there in his pants. "Excuse me." He didn't care how it must have looked to them, but he couldn't stand it.

Chastity was going to give him a damn stroke.

Chapter Six

Sebastian rushed to the men's room, grateful to see it was a one-stall unit. The last thing he needed was some curious bystander bursting in while he was handling his business. Hastily, he locked the door behind him. He unbuckled his pants before shoving an eager hand inside his boxers.

Sebastian couldn't remember a time when his dick had been so hard. As his fingers circled the rigid shaft, he sighed with relief. Never in a million years would he have thought he'd actually be driven to jerking off in a restaurant bathroom. Could there be anything more depraved?

When he finally got his hands on Chastity, he'd make her pay for the torment she was putting him through. Damn her. His fist tightened around his hardness. With a pulsing heart beating a tattoo against his chest and breath shallow, Sebastian felt like he'd die if relief didn't come soon.

Closing his eyes, he imagined pushing Chastity's thick, smooth thighs apart and sliding into her juicy pussy until all she could do was scream his name. He'd capture that scream in his mouth and taste the sweetness within. He bet she tasted like heaven. And to think, a couple months ago, she was the last person he ever thought could do this to him.

Impatient knuckles rapped against the bathroom door. Shit. "Give me a minute," he said hoarsely.

The knock repeated. "Give me a minute," he barked again.

"I think I can be of some assistance," the purring sound of a feminine voice came from the other side of the door. Chastity? Should he open the door with his cock hanging out like it was? Did he really want her to see him in this condition? Hell, this day was already weird. Why not? After all, she was the reason for his discomfort.

Sebastian stuffed his cock back inside his pants, before unlocking and wrenching the door open, only to have her push him backward. She closed the door behind her and relocked it. "Chastity, what are you doing?"

There was a half-smile on her lips and a dangerous gleam within the depths of her dark eyes. "Shut up, Sebastian," she whispered, reaching up to cup the back of his head and bringing it down to her own.

Petal soft lips moved ardently over his. Where the hell did she learn to kiss like that? Judging from the way she used to look, he wouldn't have thought she had that much experience in the sex department, but he'd been wrong before. He wasn't able to dwell on these thoughts for long because her tongue pushed its way past his lips. Goddamn she was sweet, just as he'd imagined.

Sebastian immediately wrapped his arms around the pliant body pressing against him. He reveled in the softness of her warmth. She tasted of the soft drink she'd tormented him with earlier and a unique flavor all her own. His tongue darted out to meet hers, dancing with it to the syncopated rhythm of their hearts. A burst of hot flame raced through his body, making it nearly impossible for him to stand.

Sebastian pressed his cock against the juncture of her thighs. What he really wanted was to be inside of her, but for now, he'd have to settle for what he could get. Chastity sighed softly into his mouth, letting him know just how into this she was. The way she moved her lips over his made him think she had a lot more experience than he'd originally thought. For some reason the image of her kissing other men bothered him.

A possessiveness he'd never experienced before raced through him, making Sebastian tighten his grip around her waist. He must have squeezed too tight because she tore her mouth away and gasped for breath.

"I'm sorry," he muttered, raining kisses over her face and neck.

"It's okay," Chastity groaned.

His hands slid down her back and he placed them on her plump bottom, squeezing it, trying to get as close to her as possible. "God, Chastity. You turn me on."

One eager hand reached down to grab the hem of her skirt and raised it over her thighs. She moaned, throwing her head back, exposing the smooth column of her neck. Sebastian wanted to devour her, his lips grazing the pulse of her throat. She squirmed when his fingers dipped inside her panties. He'd never been more grateful to a woman for not wearing panty hose. When his fingers found her damp, swollen button, it was like discovering heaven.

He could smell her pussy and he very badly wanted to taste it. Sebastian speared her cunt with his middle finger, sliding it in and out of her. "Yes, Sebastian. Just like that!" Chastity cried out, gripping his shoulders in a vise. Her eyes flickered open. They were clouded with desire—for him. It made Sebastian even hornier to know that he had this affect on her. She was so beautiful; he couldn't help brushing his lips against her slightly parted ones every now and then. Chastity smelled good. Really good. "The perfume you're wearing is driving me crazy. What is it?" he asked, rubbing his nose against her neck.

"Versace's Versus."

"Mmm, I like it."

"So do I," she laughed, her hand sliding down the center of his body, before pushing inside his boxers. When her fingers wrapped around his cock, he thought he'd explode. He wanted to fuck her.

While she massaged his shaft in her fist, Sebastian slid another finger into her sopping wet box. He moaned. She groaned, their hands mutually satisfying each other. "I want you. I want you so bad, Chastity, that I swear I'm going to burst." His voice was no more than a hoarse whisper.

Her fist tightened around his cock, sending tremors of delight through his body. He shook with ecstasy. A ravenous hunger for her ripped through him. Droplets of pre-come leaked from his dick and he knew an explosion would soon follow.

With an abruptness that took him by surprise, she removed her hand from his boxers. Then she grabbed his hand and yanked it from inside her panties. "Huh?" was all he could think to say. His cock ached and she was standing there in front of him adjusting her clothes. Sebastian reached out to grab her, still burning with lust.

Chastity sidestepped him, avoiding his touch.

"What the hell are you playing at, Chastity? Come here." He reached for her again, but she backed away.

"Uh-uh. Lunch time is way past over. Remember the big deal you made about my tardiness a couple months ago? We have to get back to the office."

Was she serious? "You're kidding, right? Look at me, I'm horny as hell," he groaned, gesturing to his still erect dick.

She shrugged one delicate shoulder. "Well, you seemed to be handling things just fine on your own before I showed up."

It suddenly dawned on him that she had no intention of following through. "Cock tease," he hissed.

Chastity laughed and he wanted to strangle her. "You're adorable when you don't get your way, do you know that?"

"Bitch," he said, for lack of a better word.

"But you want this bitch, don't you?" She stepped closer and planted a long, lingering kiss on his lips. "It's okay, Sebastian. I still want you too. This was just a taste of what's in store. If you're a good boy, the next time I'll give you more than just a taste." With a final pat on his cheek, she sashayed out the bathroom as if she didn't have a care in the world.

Damn if she wasn't right. He wanted her and the next time he got her alone, a taste wouldn't be enough.

ಬಿಬಿ

Chastity searched through the volumes in the law library to find the book she wanted. Months ago, if someone would have told her that she'd end up in a public restroom with Sebastian and she'd be the aggressor, Chastity would have laughed. It seemed like she had more of her mother in her than she thought.

Not knowing exactly what it was that had given her the balls to walk in on Sebastian while he was in the men's room, she was pleased with herself. Her makeover gave Chastity more confidence than she ever thought she'd possess.

No longer did she get tongue-tied whenever she talked to a good-looking man. Now she walked with a spring in her step, and her head held high. The plan was going beautifully. Actually, much better than she thought it would. It was apparent to her that Sebastian was jealous of any attention she gave to other men, as demonstrated by his reaction to Kevin, and then to Jeremy at lunch.

It hadn't been easy keeping him at arm's length these past eight weeks, but she knew the longer she pretended indifference, the crazier it would make him. She could hold him off no longer. This afternoon proved that.

The plan, however, was not completely foolproof. There was no denying how he'd made her feel. Her body had ignited with flames at his touch. She couldn't remember a time when her pussy had been wetter. He seemed to know just how to caress her in all the right places. Seduction was the name of the game, but if she kept on this path, who would be the seducer and who'd be the seduced?

So deep in her thoughts, Chastity didn't hear Jeremy enter the library until he spoke. "Chastity, fancy finding you in here."

She let out a yelp of surprise, and whirled around to glare at him. "You scared the bejesus out of me. You can't just walk up on people like that. What if I had a heart condition?"

A dark blond brow rose in question. "Do you?"

"Do I what?"

"Have a heart condition?"

"No, but that's beside the point. You didn't know if I had a medical condition or not. But if I had, you'd be feeling pretty sorry right about now."

His blue eyes gleamed wickedly. "Not if I got to give you CPR."

Chastity rolled her eyes. Jeremy was the kind of guy it was hard to stay angry with. "Behave."

"Okay. Okay. I've been duly chastised. So, what are you looking for?"

"I'm trying to find the volume with the Dumas vs. Impco case. Someone didn't put these books back in order when they took it out."

He moved to where she stood, reached up and pulled a thick, green law encyclopedia from the shelf. "Here you go, my dear."

She smiled, taking the book. "Thank you, kind sir. Well, I have to get back to my desk. I have a lot of work today. A couple people are out and it didn't help that we came back from lunch late."

"Actually, I'm glad I ran into you. We didn't really get a chance to talk like I wanted to at lunch with Sebastian there. Maybe we could do dinner instead?"

"Why?" The word flew out of her mouth before she realized how it must have sounded. She'd been questioning motives a lot lately.

"Why? Because I'd like to get to know you better and because the lunch I had planned for us, didn't quite turn out how I wanted it to."

"And you wanted it to turn out how?"

Jeremy went bright red before letting out a nervous laugh. "Well, uh, you're not going to make this easy for me, are you?"

While Chastity found Jeremy attractive with his blond hair, blue eyes, and chiseled face that could have passed for a young Paul Newman, she preferred the dark and brooding type, like Sebastian. Besides, she didn't need the added complication of getting involved with him when her focus was getting back at Sebastian.

She'd only agreed to go to lunch with him in the first place because Pearl was being particularly nasty earlier and she'd needed to get out of the office. She sighed. "Jeremy, can I be honest?"

He frowned. "You're going to give me the 'let's be friends' line, aren't you?"

"Well, it's not that I don't like you, I do, but..."

"But?"

"Well, I'm just not interested in any romantic involvement. You've always been nice to me and I appreciate it, but I can't help but wonder if you would have even thought of asking me out if I didn't have this makeover." She could tell by his reaction that she'd flustered him when he began to stammer. Chastity held up her hand to stop him. "It's okay. There's no explanation needed."

"Is it Sebastian?" When she didn't answer immediately, he rushed on. "I kind of saw the way the wind blew at lunch."

"It's not what you think."

"Isn't it? I may be slow on the uptake on certain things, but I didn't miss the state of dishevel you both returned in from the bathroom."

Heat flooded her face. Chastity was grateful that her skin tone would cover her blush. "It wasn't what you thought," she denied.

He gave her a crooked grin. "I have a feeling it's exactly what I thought. Look, if you prefer Sebastian over me, I'm okay with that. If I hadn't told you already, I really like what you've done to yourself. You can't blame a guy for trying."

She smiled back, feeling more at ease now that she knew he wouldn't push his suit. "Oh, yes I can. I'm surprised though."

"Why is that?"

"I've seen some of Sebastian's women flitting in and out of the office, so I know he likes a little variety, but I didn't know you were down with the swirl."

A confused look crossed his face. "Down with the swirl? What the heck does that mean?"

"You know, have a taste for chocolate?"

It took him a moment before understanding entered his eyes. "Oh! I get it." He chuckled. "You see? I told you I was slow on certain things. Well, to be honest, I've only dated one black woman, but that was back in college." A far-off look entered his eyes, and Chastity got the distinct impression that there was more to the story than he was letting on.

She knew it would be best to mind her own business, but curiosity got the better of her. "What happened?"

He turned his back to her with a long sigh. "It...it didn't work out. My parents..."

"Your parents didn't approve?"

"Not really. The truth of the matter is, that regardless of what my parents thought, I should have stuck by Serita's side. I was still in college though. I had it good—didn't have to get a job; my folks were paying the rent on my cushy apartment off campus and my credit card bills. To top that off, they gave me a monthly allowance as well."

"Wow, you did have it good. Your parents must be loaded."

He turned back to face her, a derisive curve on his lips. "They do okay. Anyway, when I started dating Serita, everything was wonderful until I took her home to meet the folks. They were cordial to her and smiled in her face, but I knew right away something was wrong. When she left was when they laid into me. They made it clear in no uncertain terms that if I didn't stop seeing her I'd be cut off. I...you have no idea how much I regret doing what I did next, but I broke up with her in not so nice a way."

"How old were you?"

"Nineteen. Old enough to know better."

She touched his hand in an act of understanding. "You were just a boy. We all do things in our teens that we later regret."

"I just wish I hadn't been so weak."

"You were young and scared. While I don't necessarily approve of what you did or how you did it, a lot of people would have made the same decision."

"That doesn't make it right."

"No, but at least you acknowledge your error, and that's a sign of maturity. Whatever happened to her?"

"The last time I heard, she was married with a couple of children. I guess she's happy."

"Well, things worked out for the best then."

He shrugged. "Maybe." Something in the way he said that one word made her think that all wasn't well.

"Are you still close to your parents?"

"That's the funny thing. After I dumped Serita, my relationship with my parents deteriorated. They acted as though everything was hunky-dory, but I grew to resent them to the point that I cut myself off. I realized that as long as they supported me, they could make the same threat when I did something else that didn't meet their approval. Now we only ever communicate on holidays, if that."

"That's so sad. I'm not that particularly close to my mother either, but she's still my mom and I love her."

"I love my parents too, but I just don't like them very much. Sometimes I wonder what might have been."

"Isn't that a little futile? The damage is done, and the best you can do is learn from the past."

He nodded, and then a smile appeared. "You know, I've really enjoyed this conversation with you."

"I enjoyed it too. We have to do it again sometime."

His smile widened. "Over dinner?"

Chastity laughed. "You never give up, do you?"

"I haven't even gotten started, my dear, but don't worry, I won't persist. I can take no for an answer. A word of friendly advice though, be careful with Sebastian. He's my friend, but he doesn't have the best track record with women."

Chastity smiled. "Oh, I'm not the one who'll need to be careful."

Chapter Seven

"Oh, my goodness! I can't believe you did that, girl!" Dallas screamed, falling back on the couch, her body shuddering with laughter.

"Yes, I did, and to be honest, I can hardly believe it myself. You have no idea how hard it was for me to walk away like he didn't have the same affect on me as I obviously did on him." Chastity tried hard not to remember the way his hands felt on her skin, the way his mouth slid against hers, or the thrust of his fingers in her pussy.

Sebastian's hard body pressed so deliciously against hers was all she could think about since it had happened earlier in the day. He kept giving her smoldering looks whenever he walked by her desk for the rest of the day. The tension could be cut with a knife.

Dallas squeezed her hand. "I'm so proud of you, girlfriend. Wait until we tell the guys. They'll be thrilled too."

"Yes, the plan seems to be going well. I didn't think I had it in me, but just when I find myself falling under his spell again, I think about what he said."

"That's the spirit. You should get a digital camera and take a picture of his facial expression when you drop the bomb on him."

Chastity shrugged. "And then what? Post it over the internet? No, I don't want to humiliate him to that level. As much as he's hurt me, I could never be that malevolent."

"Yet he humiliated and used you."

"He didn't realize I was listening."

"Why are you starting to make excuses for him? You're not chickening out, are you?"

"Of course not." Something still nagged her about this entire thing. It was true that he'd used her, but did Sebastian really deserve this?

Dallas pursed her lips, not looking quite convinced. "You don't sound very enthusiastic."

"I am."

"Are you really? Don't punk out on the plan now. You have to show this bastard not to toy with you again."

"I'm not backing out. I just...well, what happens if he does start having feelings for me? What if I don't have it in me to hurt him?"

Dallas crossed her arms, a shrewd look entering her dark eyes. "Is that all that's on your mind? There's something you're not telling me."

With a sigh, Chastity decided to unload completely. "I'm not sure if I can do this and not let my feelings get in the way."

"You can't be serious. After what that turkey said about you, you're still harboring feelings for him?"

"Feelings aren't like a faucet. You can't just turn them on and off, just like that. Anyway, I didn't say I had feelings for him, just that I'm not sure if I can go through with this and not get hurt. The incident in the bathroom today shook me up more than I would have liked it to."

"But then that means you have to keep reminding yourself of what a rat he is. Don't let yourself get caught up. Sure, he may be able to touch you in the right places and do things your body hasn't experienced before, but keep in mind that it's just physical and nothing more."

"But how? I'm not experienced in this like you."

"It sounds like you were doing fine to me. Is this what's really running through your mind or are you just trying to find a reason to back out?"

"I'm not trying to back out; I'm just trying to weigh all the pros and cons."

"Well, you can't end this now. I won't let you," Dallas said stubbornly.

Chastity hopped off the couch, placing hands on ample hips. "*You* won't let me?"

"You're damn right. Me and the boys put a lot of work in to give you this new look."

"Is my look what this is all about? Do you think if I halt this crusade of revenge my makeover would have been in vain? Never mind that I feel good about myself, and for the first time I don't feel like your ugly friend."

Dallas's jaw dropped. To say she looked stunned would have been an understatement. "You're not serious, are you?"

"Do I need to spell it out for you?"

"Obviously you do, because I can't believe what I'm hearing."

Chastity began to pace her living room floor. It seemed like she'd been making a lot of confessions lately. Her feelings about how she viewed herself in relation to her best friend were something she'd bottled up for a long time. She wasn't sure how to explain herself.

Taking a deep breath to calm her nerves, she walked over to the couch and took Dallas's hand in hers. "You know I love you like a sister, right?"

"Of course I do, and I love you too, girl. You've got to know that," Dallas said earnestly.

Chastity nodded. "Even though there's probably no one else I care about more, I've been jealous of you since we were kids. At times, I hated myself for feeling so petty, but I couldn't help it."

Dallas's eyes widened, the look of utter disbelief forming her lips into an "O", a range of emotions flickering in her liquid brown eyes. "Jealous of me? But why?"

"Do you really have to ask? You're gorgeous, confident and men drool when they see you. Whenever the two of us would go out, I felt like the invisible woman."

"Oh, hon, I never realized you felt that way. To me, you've always been the beautiful one."

Chastity rolled her eyes. "Yeah, right."

"Your kind of beauty comes from within. I always knew you could be stunning if you allowed yourself to be, and now you've proved me right. If the truth be told, I've always been jealous of you."

Now it was Chastity's turn to be surprised. "Me? You're pulling my leg, right?"

"I'm serious. There are so many qualities in you that I envy. You're smart, caring and people like you for the person you are. I don't have a lot of female friends because they always see me as competition. And the men...well, when they're not acting like a bunch of brainless idiots, they treat me like I'm some kind of dumb bimbo."

"I had no idea."

"The grass isn't always greener, babe. You know what I had to do to gain my independence from my family. It wasn't very pretty. It was a gritty life, and when you have only your looks to rely on, it can kill your soul."

"Thanks for sharing that with me."

Dallas flashed a set of perfect white teeth. "No biggie. Look, I didn't mean to get on your case about the Sebastian thing. It's entirely up to you whether you want to pursue this plan or not. What matters is your happiness."

Chastity was just about to give her friend a big hug when the phone rang, interrupting their moment of revelation. "Hmm, I wonder who that is," she mused, reaching out for the phone. "Hello?" Only the faint sound of breathing met her ear. "Hello?" she answered again, hoping it wasn't some sick pervert on the other end. She silently cursed herself for not checking her caller ID.

"Chastity," a deep, familiar voice filtered through the receiver. No. It couldn't be. Could it?

"Sebastian?" He'd never called her home before.

"You sound surprised. Surely you didn't think you could leave things that way between us and expect me not to seek you out."

"I didn't really give it that mu-much thought," she stammered, wishing her heart weren't beating so erratically.

"Liar." His throaty accusation cut through her thin façade.

"Look, what happened in the restroom today was a mistake. I'm sor—"

"If you tell me you're sorry, I'm going kiss you senseless the next time we see each other, which I hope will be tonight."

"Tonight?" she croaked, throat suddenly dry. "I can't."

"Why not? This is something you started, remember? Chastity, you have no idea what you did to me today. Do you know what it's like to walk around with a hard-on all day? I had to cancel the rest of my appointments because of you."

"I fail to see how that's my problem, Sebastian." She inwardly congratulated herself for managing to keep her voice level, while her body trembled all over with nerves.

"It is your problem, because I'm going to make sure you finish what you started, lady."

"Throwing down the gauntlet?"

"You'd better believe it. I've been thinking about that tight pussy all day, wondering what it would feel like wrapped around my dick."

"Sebastian—"

"You've thought about it, haven't you?"

Chastity had, but would be damned if she admitted it. "I'd rather not have this conversation right now."

He chuckled. "That's fine. There'll be other times, preferably in person. So tell me, what's going on between you and Jeremy?"

"As if I'd tell you. What's this all about anyway? Were you stood up tonight and decided to give me a call?"

"If I were seeing someone at the moment, I certainly wouldn't be on the phone playing cat and mouse with you, now would I? Damn. I must be out of my mind to even bother."

Hearing him say that was the red flag waving in front of a bull. Was he implying she wasn't worth the trouble? "Oh, trust me, I'm very much worth the bother," she retorted.

There was a pause on the other end of the line. "Prove it then. Let me take you out tonight."

"To dinner?"

"Of course."

"A little candlelight and romance? Maybe even some dancing?"

"If you'd like."

"Cut the bullshit, Sebastian. We both know what you want, and it isn't romance. You want to fuck me. I already told you before that I don't want any of that mushy stuff from you. Come to my place tonight at nine, and bring the condoms...lots of them."

A long silence followed her bold declaration. Holy crap. Did she just say that? Hardly believing her own audaciousness, she bit her lip and waited anxiously for his reply. As the quiet stretched, she began to lose her confidence. "Sebastian?" she asked tentatively, hoping he didn't hear the squeak in her voice.

"Yes. I'm still here."

"Well?"

"Is this what you really want, Chastity? I don't want you to do this and later say I coerced you. Hell, I really shouldn't get involved with one of my employees in the first place, but damn if I can walk away."

"Oh, stop being a lawyer for a minute. You're a man and I'm a woman, two consenting adults who want each other. The question is, do *you* want to do this? I could just as easily make plans with someone else."

"With whom?" he growled.

Chastity covered her mouth to stifle the laugh threatening to bubble to the surface. His jealousy was so cute. "Just a friend. Will you come or not?"

"I'll be there. This isn't some trick, is it?"

Chastity didn't realize she'd been holding her breath until she exhaled. "Of course not. You have my address right?"

"I only got your phone number from the emergency contact list. Go ahead and give me your address." After giving him the information, she wondered if this was the right thing to do. Everything just seemed so surreal. "Okay, I'll be there at nine. I'll see you then." Sebastian hung up before she could respond.

Chastity didn't know how long she sat immobile on the couch with the phone against her ear and mouth wide open with shock, but it couldn't have been very long with Dallas sitting next to her.

"Oh, my God! I can't believe you just said that to him." Her friend laughed.

She finally replaced the phone on the hook. "I can't either."

"I guess this means you're going ahead with the plan."

"I reckon it does." There was no turning back now.

෧෮෧෮෧෮

Sebastian pulled into the drugstore on the way to Chastity's. His hands shook. Shit! He hadn't been this nervous about sex since his first time with Mindy Peterson, a cute redhead he'd pursued his entire sophomore year in high school. Unfortunately, the actual event didn't live up the hype, and it wasn't until his senior year that he had sex again. Something told him though, that he wouldn't be disappointed with Chastity.

What had happened during lunch still had his body reeling. The scent, taste and feel of her sent his hormones in a tailspin. She'd left his cock so damn hard he could barely walk afterwards. Her lush body pressed enticingly against his was enough to make his balls throb with need.

He perused the condom section, wondering what kind he should purchase. Would she prefer the kind that heated up or ribbed for her pleasure? Or would his usual brand do? *Jesus H. Christ. Get a hold of yourself. You've made love to dozens of beautiful women.* This was Chastity Bryant for Pete's sake.

The woman had him twisted in knots.

"Damn," he muttered to himself, finally deciding to get the usual brand.

"Very nice," a husky feminine voice said next to him.

He turned his head to see an attractive brunette with big green eyes smiling at him. Wearing a tube top and a micro-mini that barely covered her crotch, she was just a little too obvious for his taste. Sebastian gave the *lady* a brief smile, He made a move to walk by her, but she ran a finger down the side of his arm.

"Can I help you?" he asked, stealing a quick glance at his watch. He really needed to get back on the road if he wanted to get to Chastity's on time. He wanted to give her as little opportunity as possible to change her mind.

"You're not going to use all those tonight, are you?"

He lifted a brow. Was this broad kidding? Something definitely wasn't on the up and up. "If things go as planned, I will." Sebastian tried to pass her again, but she blocked his way.

"That's too bad, because I can show you things that your date tonight couldn't imagine."

This woman was obviously a prostitute. Why him? Disgust washed through him. "No thank you. I'm fine."

"You don't know what you're missing, baby."

"I said I was fine, thank you," he said more firmly.

"I can take you to heaven, baby," she persisted, boldly reaching out to trail her finger down the front of his pants.

Sebastian backed up. "Hookers are not my thing. Now if you don't mind, I'd like to get by, please."

"A girl's gotta earn a living, but no one turns down Lola. Are you gay or something?"

He could have very well said something mean, but decided that if pretending he was gay would get this pariah off his back, then he'd do it. "Uh, yeah, that's it. I'm gay."

To his astonishment, instead of walking away, she grinned, revealing a slight overbite. "Why didn't you say so, baby. I got what you need." Lifting her skirt, the brunette showed off a large bulge in her panties.

Sebastian wanted to hurl. Great. Out of all the drugstores he could have stopped at along the way, he had to choose the one with a transvestite trolling the aisles, looking for action. He pushed past the she-male, dropping the box of condoms. To hell with them, he'd go somewhere else.

Sebastian only hoped that with all he'd been through on this weird day, that Chastity would make it all better.

Chapter Eight

Chastity paced her living room floor, creating a trail in her plush cream carpet. Monty's head followed her movements across the room as if he were watching a tennis match. She still couldn't believe she'd issued an invitation for Sebastian to come over. Did she have the guts to go through with this?

Wrapping her arms around her body to still the shivers, she wondered if wearing this ridiculously see-through nightgown was a good idea. Nick and Kevin had talked her into buying a couple of sexy night things. The lilac gossamer nightgown she currently sported had looked sexy in the store, but on her body, it seemed indecent. She felt downright naked.

Dallas had bullied her into wearing it for Sebastian's arrival. Chastity looked over at the standing full-length mirror on her living room floor, allowing her arms to fall to her sides. She twisted and turned, examining her body. Hanging by two spaghetti straps, the gown nearly touched the floor and hugged her voluptuous curves. The slits on the sides allowed her to move freely.

Her hair rested in a dark cloud around her shoulders and her make-up was freshly repaired. She had to admit that she did feel pretty, but what would Sebastian think? Self-consciously, she touched her rounded belly knowing she'd never be model slim, but right now it didn't seem to matter.

The insistent buzz of the doorbell announced Sebastian's arrival.

"Come on, girl, you can do this," she whispered. Taking a quick look through her peephole before answering, she opened the door with a smile on her face. "Sebastian, you're right on time." Her heart banged against her breast nearly making it impossible to breathe, when he entered her house.

She was so used to seeing him in suits and ties, that his casual appearance almost made her swoon. He wore a black crew-neck shirt that looked great against his olive skin and showed off his sinewy arms to perfection. Tufts of black hair peeked out of his shirt, enhancing his masculinity.

His blue jeans were so indecently tight that she could see the outline of his cock. Sparks of merriment danced in his green eyes. "Have you had your fill, or would you like for me to turn around so you can check out my ass too?"

Chastity's face grew hot. How long had she been staring at the bulge in his pants? She gulped, remembering how thick his cock had felt when she'd wrapped her fingers around it. Embarrassed at being caught out, she tried to channel the confidence she'd felt earlier. "You don't have to turn around. I've seen that ass walk by my desk on several occasions."

"And did you like what you saw?"

"Oh, yeah"

Sebastian grinned. "Good. Because I like what I'm seeing now. You look very sexy."

"Thanks. You don't look too shabby yourself. Those jeans should be outlawed."

He chuckled, handing her a bottle of wine. "This is for you."

She took it with nerveless fingers. "I appreciate this, but you didn't have to bring me anything."

"I know I didn't have to, but I was raised to bring a gift to the hostess whenever I'm invited to someone's house for the first time."

"That's awful sweet of you, Sebastian, but we both know what you came here for," she said with bravado.

"Maybe so, but that wouldn't excuse a lack of manners. Now, just say thank you."

"Thank you."

"Actually, my motive wasn't completely altruistic. I'm hoping you'll share a glass with me."

By now his gaze was slowly devouring her body, sliding up and down her curves. She grew warm under his perusal. Biting her lower lip, Chastity pressed her thighs tightly together to temper the surging heat within.

"Don't do that, Chastity, unless you want me to throw you on the ground right here and now. It drives me crazy when you nibble on your lip like that, because I want to be the one doing the nibbling. Go pour us a couple glasses of wine, and I'll put on some music. Where do you keep your CDs?"

Soundlessly she pointed in the direction of her CD rack before scurrying out of the living room to the kitchen, her pulse racing. This was supposed to be her seduction scene, so why did Sebastian have to be so calm when her knees felt like they'd give out any second?

Steadying her shaking hands, Chastity poured two glasses of wine and took a sip from one to soothe her nerves. Just as she stepped into the living room, the phone rang. Who in the world could that be calling at this time of night?

Sebastian looked slightly annoyed. "Ignore it."

"I can't. It might be an emergency." She very well could have ignored it, but she needed to buy some time to build up her courage again. "Hello?" she answered, a little more breathlessly than she intended.

"Chas, it's Kevin."

"Kevin, you're calling at a bad time. I have company now."

"I know. Dallas called and told us what's going on and we saw Mr. Stud Muffin pull up in your driveway. He's hot."

"Okay. If you know it's a bad time, then why are you calling?" she whispered, taking a peek over her shoulder. Sebastian's face was screwed up in a scowl. His displeasure was obvious.

"I called to give the appearance that he's not the only one you might be seeing."

"Lord have mercy. You've been hanging around Dallas way too much. Look, I really have to go, but I'll talk to you tomorrow."

"Okay. Are we still on for shopping this weekend? There's a killer sale at Macy's."

"Yes, we're still on. I'll see you then." Clicking the phone off, she replaced it on the receiver. If Sebastian was upset before, he looked positively dangerous now; his normally pale eyes a murky, dark green and his lips a thin, angry line. "I'm sorry about that."

She slid next to him on the couch, figuring that not mentioning the phone conversation would be the best way to handle things. Sebastian, on the other hand, wasn't willing to let it go so easily. "Who...was...that?" he asked as though struggling to get each word out.

She shrugged, trying to project an air of nonchalance she didn't feel. "Just a friend."

"What kind of friend?" he demanded.

When Sebastian's eyes bored into her, he reminded Chastity of Othello, right before he strangled Desdemona. *Thanks a lot, Kevin.* She could have dragged this out and make it seem like Kevin and her were more to each other than what they were, but judging by the look on his face, Chastity realized that wasn't a good idea. There was only so far a man like Sebastian could be pushed.

"The platonic kind. If I didn't know better, I'd think you were jealous."

"Maybe I am."

His admission took Chastity by surprise. Not quite knowing how to respond, she changed topics. "So, what do you think about my nightgown. You didn't say anything about it when you walked in."

"I said you looked sexy. Isn't that the same thing?" He laughed, visibly relaxing, which in turn, relaxed her.

I can do this, she silently chanted. "Not quite the same thing, but I guess I'll let you slide this time."

Sebastian scooted closer. Her body ignited when his hip touched hers. Chastity's breath caught in her throat. God, he was gorgeous. It just didn't seem fair for one man to be so damn hot.

He ran a finger down her chest to where her nightgown dipped. "I like what you're wearing very much, but I bet I'll enjoy it even more when I'm taking it off. Of course, you know, I'm the only one you're allowed to wear this for now."

Chastity trembled. Was it her or did the temperature in her house just go up? "I'll keep that in mind," she said unsteadily.

"You'd better," he growled. "You have no idea what I went through before I got here."

She raised an eyebrow. "And what was it that you went through that was so grueling."

"Well, I nearly got a ticket racing over here, but the poor officer took pity on me when I told her that I had to go see a friend in need."

Chastity pursed her lips. "She? You charmed your way out of a ticket, you mean? What a hardship."

"And, I had to fend off a transvestite prostitute when I stopped to purchase condoms on the way here."

"You're making that up."

"I swear, I'm telling you the truth. From my mouth to God's ears."

This made her laugh. "That's what you get for being so darn irresistible. I bet everything comes easy to you. You always do what you like, don't you?"

"If I had done what I really wanted to when I walked in here, you would have thought I was an animal."

She saw her opportunity to flip the script on him and took it. Leaning over, Chastity brushed his lips with hers. "It's okay. I like animals." The tips of her breasts grazed his arm. She pressed another kiss against his jaw, her hand slowly inching up his thigh.

Sebastian suddenly pulled back. "We're really going to do this, right? No turning back this time?"

"Of course. Isn't this what you wanted?"

"More than you know, but..."

"But what?"

"You're a totally different person. I never know what to expect. With the old Chastity, I could read you like a book, but now you go hot and the next minute cold. I don't want to get all worked up again, just to be left high and dry."

"I plan to see this through. I want you as much as you want me."

"What happened to you, anyway?"

Was he serious? Sebastian was the one who'd made her realize what a hopeless mouse she'd been. He almost sounded like he missed the mouse. Well that was just too damn bad. The reminder of her former self gave Chastity the strength to make her next move. "I finally opened my eyes...thanks to you." She reached over and cupped his face in her hands. "I don't know about you, but I want to fuck." And with that she crushed his lips beneath hers.

ಜಜಜ

Chastity's sweet mouth covered his in an aggressive, hungry kiss. Sebastian's initial reaction was to push her away and find out what she'd meant by that last comment, but her soft lips roaming so urgently against his shattered all intentions to smithereens.

He wrapped his arms around her warm, voluptuous body. When Chastity had opened the door, he'd nearly dropped the bottle of wine in his hand, almost losing the control he's fought so hard to maintain when he saw Chastity in her pitiful excuse for a nightgown.

He could make out the blackberry colored nipples that pressed against the flimsy material of her bodice and his mouth went dry. She wasn't wearing underwear either; the dark patch of hair that rested enticingly between her thick thighs tempted him to his limits. Absolutely gorgeous.

Sebastian congratulated himself when he didn't toss her on the ground and screw her senseless. He wasn't completely sure if he believed this Kevin person was the platonic friend she claimed. He sensed there was something deeper there. He fully intended to find out exactly what that was, but right now, nothing mattered beyond how wonderful her lips felt and how good she smelled.

Chastity's tongue pushed forward, tracing the outline of his mouth. Sebastian's lips parted under her gentle assault. Just as he remembered, she tasted tangy and sweet at once. He couldn't recall the last time a woman had made him feel this urgent need. His cock was harder than it had ever been before.

Tightening his arms around her abundant body, Sebastian wanted to be as close to her as possible. Her tongue stroked his, circling and sucking it into her mouth. He groaned at the delicious stimulation. Normally he was the one in charge when sex was involved, but Chastity was sending him a clear message. She was piloting this plane.

His internal heat index rose, beads of sweat breaking out on his forehead. She kissed like a highly trained courtesan and again, Sebastian wondered where she'd learned such a skill. Pulling apart from her a bit, he grazed her jawline with his mouth.

"You're beautiful," he whispered against her skin. And he meant it. His voluptuous, beautiful paralegal made his dick ache in ways he didn't think possible. He trailed kisses down the side of her neck.

"Oh, Sebastian, that feels wonderful." She moaned.

"I can make you feel even better, baby." She shivered under his butterfly caresses. Fingers dug through his hair and pulled his head against her body.

Inhaling the sweet scent of her perfume, he rubbed his face on the tops of her breasts. Unable to wait any longer, he slid the straps of the gown from her smooth brown shoulders. The negligee fell into a pool at her waist to reveal a pair of large chocolate breasts, capped with huge areolas and the darkest, most succulent nipples he'd ever laid eyes on.

Sebastian couldn't wait to taste them. Though they drooped slightly from the sheer weight, they were firm and well shaped. "They're beautiful," he murmured, cupping them in his palms. He rubbed his thumbs over the pouty peaks. Chastity trembled, a soft sigh tumbling from her lips. It pleased him to see how turned on she was.

Sebastian lifted the large mounds to his descending mouth. He laved one pert tip, licking and swirling it, before capturing it between his teeth.

"Sebastian," Chastity groaned, tightening the grip she had in his hair. When he flicked the hardened point with his tongue again, she writhed against him, squirming as though she couldn't keep still. He lifted his head to stare into passion-glazed eyes.

"Do you like this, Chastity? Do you like the feel of my mouth on you?"

"You know I do."

"How would I know unless you tell me?" he asked, tracing her aureoles with shaking fingers. "I want you to tell me how much you like this. Tell me how much you want me." Bending his head, he kissed the valley of her breasts.

Chastity's sharp intake of breath told him just how much she did in fact want him, and though actions should have been enough, he needed the validation of her words. Weeks ago, Sebastian knew that he only had to mention something and she'd practically fall over herself to do his bidding. Now, he could never be sure of what she would say.

It wasn't that he wanted her to hang on his every word again, but he sort of missed the sweet woman with her ready compliments. This new Chastity sent shockwaves of ecstasy through his veins, but parts of him couldn't help wondering what happened. She made him feel so unsure, a feat no woman had ever accomplished.

When she didn't immediately answer, he pinched each nipple between his fingers, tweaking them until she cried out. "Tell me that you want me. I want to hear you say it."

"I want you."

"Say my name."

"Sebastian," she whispered obediently.

"Say, I want you, Sebastian. Tell me how much you want me," he commanded, applying more pressure to her nipples.

She gasped. "I want you, Sebastian. I want you so bad it hurts. I ache for you."

"Tell me what you want me to do about it."

Desire blazed within the depths of her eyes. "I want you to fuck me," Chastity answered breathlessly.

Sebastian smiled, smugness flowing through him. He knew he had Chastity where he wanted her and now he was the one in control. "Uh-uh. You don't get off so easily, baby." He licked the curve of her shoulder. "I want you to tell me in detail what you want me to do to you."

"Why? I thought this was what you wanted too." Her voice sounded tremulous and unsure. Good. Now she was the one in a tailspin.

"Because, sometimes a guy needs to hear these things."

"Okay, but only if you take your shirt off too."

When he yanked his top off, she immediately placed her hands against his bare chest. "Nice," she whispered. He closed his eyes briefly, savoring her touch. Sebastian looked down at her hands against his body; the contrast of her dark, delicately shaped fingers splayed against his much lighter skin was an erotic sight to behold. He didn't realize something so simple could turn him on like this. Capturing her hands in his, he shook his head.

"Oh, no you don't. I hope you didn't think I'd let you off the hook after what happened this afternoon. So now, as your punishment, I want you to tell me what you want from me and don't leave out a single detail."

"Isn't it enough that I said how much I want you?"

Sebastian raised the hem of her nightgown, sliding it up the length of her thighs. He pried her legs apart and brushed his knuckles against the tight curls nestled over her pussy. Chastity released a stilted breath. "Isn't it?" she asked again.

"Not by a long shot, babe."

He parted her damp slit and slipped his middle finger into her channel. She was so fucking wet. And tight. She'd fit like a glove around his cock. Chastity bucked her hips against his hand. "Sebastian, please."

"Oh, I intend to, but first you're going to tell me what I want to hear."

"I want you inside of me."

"Sebastian."

"Huh?"

"Say my name when you speak to me. I don't want you to confuse me with your friend Kevin."

"But he's—"

"Spare me. Just tell me what I need to hear," he demanded, sliding another finger inside her, rubbing his thumb against her blood-engorged clit.

Her body shook with apparent pleasure. "I want you to put your cock inside of me...Sebastian. I want your hands on my breasts, my pussy and ass—everywhere. I want your mouth against my skin. Now stop torturing me and give me what we both want. I can't take this anymore." Her voice was no more than a harsh whisper.

Sebastian removed his now dew soaked fingers, her scent clinging to them. Then he licked them, watching her reaction. "Mmm, delicious. You should have a taste," he said, rubbing those very same fingers against Chastity's bottom lip.

"Go ahead. Taste how flavorful you are."

Tentatively, she opened her mouth around his still wet digits before closing her lips around them. The gentle way her tongue swayed back and forth as she sucked him made his dick ache and balls throb.

He didn't know how much longer he'd be able to hold out before revealing how he burned for her. She nibbled on his fingers, moaning around them as if it were his cock. Sebastian looked into the liquid pools of her eyes just as Chastity pulled her head back and ran the tip of her tongue over her lips.

She smiled, revealing deep dimples. "You're right. I am delicious."

He grinned reaching over to pick up a glass of wine before dipping his index finger inside of it. Then, he circled a turgid nipple and captured the wine soaked peak in his mouth, sucking greedily.

"Oh, Sebastian, you're going to be the death of me," she moaned.

He repeated the motion with her other breast. The taste of wine against her skin titillated his taste buds. His goal was to reduce her to a quivering mass of flesh. Looking into her dazed eyes, he knew he'd succeeded.

Impatiently, he replaced the wine glass and scooped her off the sofa.

"Sebastian, put me down. I'm too heavy."

"Shut up, Chastity. Just point me to the direction of your bedroom."

Wordlessly, she pointed toward the stairs. Sebastian's mouth watered in anticipation when he dropped her unceremoniously on the bed. He intended to make this a night she wouldn't soon forget.

Chapter Nine

Chastity lay on the bed, trembling uncontrollably. How had he been able to turn the tables on her so easily? One minute she was in charge and the next he had her panting for him like a bitch in heat. At first she'd been self-conscious of how he'd view her body with so little clothes, but when Sebastian bared her breasts before his hungry gaze, she'd never felt more desirable.

Now, here she was on the center of the bed with a fire blazing a trail from her head to her feet. She watched him undress, her breath unsteady. With each article of clothing discarded, Sebastian revealed his lean, lightly muscled physique. He was all taut lines and hard planes. The beautiful symmetry of his body would have made Mr. Universe jealous.

Chastity's eyes widened at the sight of Sebastian's cock as he slid his boxers down lean hips. It was slightly above average in length, but the thickness...holy shit he was thick. The blunt, mushroom-shaped head crowning his dick was a deep shade of pink, a drop of pre-come glistening from the tip. She wanted to catch the murky dollop with her tongue.

She didn't realize how hard she was staring until Sebastian cleared his throat, grabbing her attention. Her eyes slowly trailed up the length of his toned torso. He was magnificent and for now, he was all hers. How many times had she dreamed of this moment?

"Do you like what you see?" he asked, wrapping his hand around the stiff rod. He bent down, lifted his pants and pulled out a condom. Chastity watched in fascination, her breath growing shallow, as he slid the rubber slowly over his hard length. Her fingers itched to caress him and stroke his cock within her eager hand.

Sebastian slid his fist back and forth over his erection, making her mouth go dry. Chastity wished she knew what was going on in his head. It seemed like he was in a teasing mood. If that were the case, two could play at that game. She eased her nightgown over her hips and tossed it aside. Positioning herself on the side, she circled one tight nipple, poking out her bottom lip as provocatively as possible.

"Sebastian, it's getting cold over here. Don't you want to join me?"

He smirked. "Only if you ask nicely, babe," he said with a husky whisper, his masturbatory motions slowing slightly. She was getting to him.

Chastity raised an eyebrow. "You're going to make me beg for it, huh?"

"Oh yeah."

"It is rather tempting and your cock looks rather delicious, but it also looks like it's very lonely. My pussy will keep it company." Letting her lashes fall, she lay on her back and spread her legs. Cupping her hand over her aching sex, Chastity rubbed the sensitive mound back and forth. Her other hand continued to fondle her breast, before sliding down her belly.

Chastity touched the damp slit of her entrance, her eyes locking with Sebastian's. She was so hot, touching herself while he watched. The look of unbridled passion burning in his green gaze gave her the courage to be this bold. The exhibitionist was out in full force, a side of her she didn't realize she had.

Sebastian's fists were now clenched tightly by his sides, his dick shooting forward. He gnashed his teeth together with apparent frustration. She'd laugh if she could, but held her mirth in. Chastity parted her labia, lifting her hips so he could get a better view. She enjoyed watching his control slowly slip away as she touched herself in ways she'd never allowed anyone to see before.

"Sebastian, I wish you would come over and join me, but if you'd prefer to stand over there, I guess I'll have to get myself off. Mmm," she groaned, riding her hand. She licked her lips seductively.

"Chastity," he hissed, but she closed her eyes, shutting out the sight of him. Inserting two fingers in her hot pussy, she imagined Sebastian's cock there instead. She wished he'd stop being so stubborn. Chastity didn't have to wait long before she heard his impassioned curse.

Her eyes popped open just in time to see him storming over, his dick bobbing with each angry step. "Damn you, woman. I'll teach you to tease me."

The bed depressed under his weight and he grabbed her wrists before pinning them above her head. Then he covered her body with his. Holding her still with one hand, he used the other one to part her cunt for his entrance.

Slamming into her with one forceful thrust, his balls slapped against her ass. "Oh, God!" she screamed at the delectable feeling of being wonderfully stretched by his thick cock.

"He can't help you. You're mine now." He moaned. "Damn you're tight. It's like this pussy was made just for me."

Sebastian nipped the side of her neck just where it connected to her shoulder. Chastity was filled with a primitive need to be claimed and branded by this man, her body shaking with each kiss he rained over her face and throat.

"Tell me how much you want me again." He pushed powerfully into her.

"I want you very badly." To prove her point, Chastity wrapped her thighs around his hips, sucking his dick deeper into her slippery channel. A wave of unadulterated lust swept through her, igniting a burning flame. "Yes! Yes! Yes! I want it harder, faster!" she cried out.

"Say my name."

"Sebastian."

"Louder goddammit! It's the least you owe me for bringing me to this." He rammed his cock into her with animalistic urgency.

"Sebastian!" she screamed, trying to break free of his iron clad grip. More than anything she wanted to touch him, to feel him beneath her palms. "Let go of my wrists."

A rough laugh tore from his throat. "Not on your life, babe. If I let you touch me, this will be over before it can even begin."

Chastity sighed, knowing there was no winning this argument. Closing her eyes, she allowed herself to let go and revel in the thunderous pounding of his dick slipping in and out of her, binding them together.

She bucked her hips up, meeting him thrust for thrust. If she couldn't touch him, then she would at least give as good as she got. Their mating was frantic and rapturous, like two people in desperate need of each other. Sweat-slicked bodies glided together until a slow, steady build up filled the pit of her stomach. It rapidly spread to every single nerve ending in her body, rocking Chastity to the core.

Sebastian plowed into her cunt, taking her to a peak so intense, she screamed. Finally, he released her wrists and she ran her nails down his back, breaking skin. "Oh, God! Sebastian!" An overwhelming explosion sliced through her, unlike anything she'd ever experienced before. Chastity started to shake and couldn't stop. Sebastian strained against her, signaling his own climax.

With ragged breath, he fell on top of her. "Chastity, I never knew it could be like this," he whispered against her heated skin.

"Neither did I," she whispered back. And this worried her. What she'd felt for him before was just a crush, but knowing how sexually compatible they were and experiencing such mind-blowing pleasure at his hands, she realized her heart could very easily become engaged.

Unable to think properly with his arms curled so tightly around her, she made a move to pull away. He squeezed her tighter. "Oh, no you don't. You're not going anywhere."

"Don't...don't you have to leave soon?"

His pale eyes darkened. "Trying to get rid of me already? Do you have another lover lined up at midnight?"

"No, it's not that. I just figured you'd want to leave soon because it's a work night."

"I'm well aware of that, but we have time. Just let me hold you for a little while."

She was taken by surprise at his reluctance to leave. She never took Sebastian for a cuddler. Making one last attempt to break free, she said, "Well, I need my rest and if I'm going to get up on time, I'll need to go to sleep now."

"Then go to sleep."

"But—"

Sebastian cut her off, pressing his lips against hers. The slow, languid kiss made her tingle all over. "Go to sleep."

She could have insisted that he leave, but the truth was, she didn't want him to. Chastity snuggled against his warmth. As she drifted to sleep, she thought of how good his arms felt around her.

శంశంశం

Something woke him up. Disoriented, Sebastian looked around. Where the hell was he? Feeling a warm body next to his, he suddenly remembered. This was Chastity's bedroom. He could smell the scent of their mingled sex in the air.

It hadn't been a dream. Now there was no going back, but he wasn't sure he wanted to. Granted, it was a sticky situation getting involved with an employee, but he could no more walk away from her than a thirsty man from a glass of water. The sex had been earth-shattering. Nothing had prepared him for this.

Looking over at Chastity's sleeping form curled so snuggly under the covers, she looked so vulnerable. She reminded him of a sleeping angel, her dark hair fanned out against the stark white pillow and long lashes practically resting on her cheeks. She looked so peaceful he had to strain in order to hear her soft, even breathing. One hand lay under her head, cupping her cheek.

He bent over and brushed his lips against her temple. Sebastian's cock stirred. Just a mere touch and he was rendered horny. She must have put a spell on him or something. Why else would he feel this way, after fucking her not so long ago.

When they'd made this date, Sebastian suspected it would be good between them, but what happened exceeded his wildest expectations. Now that he'd had her, once wasn't enough. He wanted more.

A warm swash of fur slid over his arm. He jumped. What the hell? Two pairs of glowing yellow eyes stared back at him. Chastity's cats. Chuckling to himself, he released a sigh of relief. "You two mongrels don't belong up here." When he reached to lift the closest feline off the bed, it swiped an angry paw at him.

"Shit! You little monster!" he hissed, rubbing his injured hand.

"What's going on?" Chastity rose slowly into a sitting position. She rubbed her eyes and looked over at him. "Sebastian." The way she said his name almost sounded like she was surprised to see him there. "What happened?"

"Your damn cat scratched me."

"Oh, no! I'm really sorry about that. Monty doesn't particularly care for strangers and you are sleeping on the side of the bed he usually occupies." She shooed the two cats off the bed.

If Sebastian didn't know better, he would have said the cat who'd taken a swipe at him glared before jumping off. "So, you sleep with those fleabags every night?"

"Be nice. They have feelings, you know."

"Don't tell me you're one of those weird cat ladies."

Chastity giggled. "Well, if loving my cats makes me a weird cat lady, then I guess I am. I'm not ashamed of my feelings for them."

Something in her tone caught him off guard. "I meant no offense."

"None taken. Just letting you know. I see you're holding on to your hand. Is this where he scratched you?" It didn't escape his notice how quick she was to change the subject. She picked up his hand in hers.

"It's fine."

"No, it's not. This welt feels pretty nasty. Get up and I'll clean it for you." Sliding out of bed, she walked over to her closet.

Sebastian admired her generous backside, the rounded curve making his dick harder than it already was. He licked his lips in anticipation of another go round with her. Chastity had the kind of ass rappers glamorized. The next time they fucked, he'd take her from behind, and maybe she'd let him slide his cock between those luscious cheeks. Just the thought of slamming into that succulent ass made him spring out of bed.

He walked up behind her just as she pulled out a robe. Wrapping his arms around her waist, he nuzzled her neck.

She moaned. "What are you doing, Sebastian?"

"I want you again," he murmured, pressing kisses on her skin, as he rubbed his erection against her bottom.

"But your hand—"

"Forget about it. I told you it was fine."

"It could get infected though." Cupping her large breasts in his palms, he ran his thumbs over puckered nipples. Chastity's head fell back against his chest. "You don't play fair."

"Neither do you. Have you any idea what you did to me these past couple months? I'd say some payback was in order." He let one chocolate mound go to trail his hand down her stomach before sliding two fingers into her still wet pussy. "Ride my hand."

Her hips gyrated up and down come-drenched fingers. Reaching up to encircle his neck, Chastity held his head close to her face, their lips meeting. Sebastian's tongue poked out to greet hers, circling and entwining with it in a sensual dance of seduction.

A raging inferno spread throughout his body, threatening to incinerate him on the spot. He knew she felt it too by the way she trembled against him. "That's it, baby. Don't hold back."

She moved up and down, her ass brushing his cock. Sebastian wanted so badly to take his dick and push it past her tight anal ring. The very thought of it gave him such a head rush that his entire body shook.

"Harder," she whispered, writhing against him. He fucked her with quick hard strokes, jamming his fingers into her tight hole as deep as they'd go. The soft, sweet moans she emitted intensified his lust for her.

Bending over, he nipped her earlobe, tugging it with his teeth. There wasn't any part of her he didn't want to explore. The fragrant smell of her pussy filled his nostrils. God, he ached. Chastity tightened her arm around his neck and screamed his name. "Sebastian! I'm coming!" A warm flow of her honey drenched his hand, but he wasn't through with her yet.

He wanted that ass.

Slowly easing his finger out of her sopping cunt, he slid them between her plump cheeks. She tensed. "Relax, Chastity. I just want to play with you," he whispered against her ear, sliding his fingers along her tight anus.

"I don't like that," she protested, a hint of fear in her voice.

"Has anyone ever done this to you before?"

"No, but it's not right."

"What's not right about it? We're two consenting adults. You can't say you don't like something unless you've tried it."

Still sliding his finger against the puckered bud, he kissed her neck.

"Will you at least try?" Sebastian kissed her soft flesh again. "For me?"

"But what if it hurts?"

"Then I'll stop. Relax. Let me in, baby." He pushed his middle finger gently into her rectum.

"Oh!"

"Relax. Let your body go." He withdrew just until it reached the tip, and then pushed it back in again. He repeated the motion several times before she moaned. "Do you like this?"

"I'm not sure...it is starting to feel rather nice," she whispered with stilted breath.

"Good, because I like doing it to you."

Chastity yelped when he added another finger inside her ass.

"Sebastian," she sighed, contentment evident in her voice.

"That's it, baby. This ass was meant for fucking. You may not be ready now, but next time, I'm going to use my cock. Do you masturbate?" he asked, not stopping the rhythm of his fingers.

She nodded.

"The next time you're alone lying in your bed, I want you to think of me. I want you to get that pussy nice and wet. Then, I want you to slide a finger into your ass. I want you to prepare yourself for my cock. Will you do that for me?"

"Yes, just don't stop!"

"Oh, don't worry. I won't. This night is just beginning." Sebastian pumped his hand against her until she came again, her body slumping weakly against his. "Where's your bathroom?"

"The door to the left."

Sebastian led her inside and turned the shower tap to hot. Guiding her under the warm spray, he pulled her close to him.

Chastity moaned. "Mmm, this feels good, but it's going to take forever to dry my hair."

"Don't worry. I'll do it for you."

She lifted one perfectly arched brow. "Oh yeah, and what do you know about doing hair?"

"Not a lot, but I'm pretty nifty with a blow dryer and I know how much I enjoy running my fingers through your hair."

"I just may have to take you up on that offer." She yawned, resting her head against his chest. "Oh, my. I'm not going to want to go to work tomorrow."

"Then take the day off. You have my permission."

"I don't expect special privileges just because I'm fucking the boss." The offhanded way in which she said it annoyed him.

"I'm not giving you special privileges. I'm simply giving you my permission to stay home if you'd like. You haven't taken a day off, probably since you've worked for the firm to my knowledge. Don't be so damn touchy."

"I just—"

"Chastity, shut up," he said, before covering her mouth with his. She made the entire thing sound so sordid and he didn't like it one bit.

He realized then just how easily he could get in over his head.

Chapter Ten

Sebastian pulled up to his mother's driveway. Taking deep breaths, he readied himself for the onslaught. Normally when she quizzed him about his love life and when he'd settle down, he'd laugh it off and change the subject. This time, he wasn't sure how he'd answer her.

It had been a month since that first time with Chastity and he still didn't know where he stood with her. Three nights out of the week he went to her apartment and the sex was fantastic. His body would react to her diligent caresses in ways he didn't think were possible.

Whenever she was near, his cock immediately jumped to attention, which made for some embarrassing moments at the office. Yet, he wasn't satisfied with the way things were between them. At work, she was all business, which was fine with him, but other times when he tried to get closer she wouldn't let him in.

Chastity always had an excuse not to get together with him on the weekends and she never shared anything about her life except for brief glimpses. It frustrated the hell out of him. Despite that, he found himself wanting to be with her. His thoughts were consumed by her. Chastity had him twisted in knots and he was slowly losing his mind.

Eve Vaughn

Marina Rossi came out of the front door, a large smile on her face. His mother was pushing fifty, but didn't look a day over thirty-five. Her lovely face was framed by coal black hair she got touched up monthly and she had a slender, petite frame that had men half her age hitting on her.

Sebastian often wondered why his mother never remarried. It certainly wasn't from lack of offers.

"Come on in. I have some meatballs cooking and they're almost ready."

Walking over to his mother, he lifted her in a huge bear hug and kissed her cheek. She laughed. "Put me down, you big lug."

When he set her on the ground he looked down into green eyes so like his own. "How are you, Mama?"

"I'm great, but it would seem I should be asking you that question. Tell me, what's wrong?"

He swore the woman had to be part witch to read him so well. "There's nothing wrong at all. Just that I miss you."

"Well, your visits have become few and far between lately, but I understand how busy you get sometimes, dear."

Sebastian sighed as he followed her into the house. Here it comes, he thought with a sense of doom. Settling down in her favorite spot to chat, the kitchen table, he tried to steer the conversation away from where he knew she'd want to take it. "Those meatballs smell good. Do you need me to help prepare anything?"

His mother shot him a knowing look. "You know I don't like anyone messing around my kitchen. Something's on your mind, son. I saw it the minute you stepped out of your car. Why don't you tell me what's going on?"

He knew his mother would get it out of him sooner or later, so what was the point of prevaricating? "Things at work are great. The firm is expanding and we're looking to bring a few more attorneys on board."

She shrugged. "Okay. That still doesn't answer my question, although I'm delighted about your success. Is everything okay with your sister? That girl doesn't call me half as much as she should."

"No. Robin's great. I saw her a couple days ago. She's making lots of friends, so she doesn't want big brother hovering around. You need to relax about her. She's not a baby anymore."

"But her disability—"

"If she doesn't let it stop her, then we shouldn't either. She's doing fine."

Marina sighed, wistfully. "I suppose you're right. It's hard to believe all my babies have lives of their own. Your brother is thinking about opening his own practice."

Sebastian smirked, thinking of his younger brother Michael, who was now a bona fide doctor. It didn't surprise him one bit that Mike chose to specialize in Obstetric and Gynecology, considering he used to go around giving the neighborhood girls free breast exams when they were kids. Mike had, of course, matured a great deal since then and Sebastian was very proud of him. "That's good news. I'll have to give him a call this week."

"It sometimes feels like you three don't need me anymore."

Sebastian took his mother's hand in his. "I hope you know that we'll always need you."

She smiled. "You're sweet for saying that. Now stop trying to change the subject and tell me what's going on."

"I'm...sort of been seeing someone."

This was obviously something his mother wasn't expecting. "Did I hear you correctly? Did you say you're involved with someone? Oh, thank God! My prayers have been answered." She threw her arms in the air. "When can I meet her? What's she like? Is she a nice Italian girl? Is she Catholic?"

"Calm down, Mama. I've only been with her for a month and technically we're not really together. If the truth be known, I'm not exactly sure what we are."

His mother's eyebrows furrowed together in consternation. "I'm not sure I understand."

"That's the problem. I don't understand either. You see, she's actually one of my employees."

"Oh, Sebastian, you have to be careful with that. I just saw a movie about a guy who got involved with a co-worker. When he tried to end it, she goes berserk. I'd hate for that to happen to you."

Sebastian shook his head. "First of all, you really should lay off the trashy movies, and second, this situation is unique."

"I may not be as worldly as you, but I know a few things, so watch your tone with me, mister. All I'm saying is to be careful."

Squeezing the hand he held, Sebastian nodded.

"You're right, Mama, and I apologize for my tone. However, my problem is a little different. Not very long ago, this woman was a workhorse. She still works very hard, but all the extra stuff she used to do, she doesn't anymore."

"Why do you think she stopped?"

"I don't know, but around that time, she sort of changed. Her attitude, and then her appearance. I had no idea the caterpillar was actually a stunning butterfly."

"And let me guess, that's when you started to take notice?"

"Well, yes—I mean no."

His mother lifted a brow, shooting him a yeah right look.

"Let me explain. It's true that I never saw her as more than just a diligent employee, but once she changed, I've never been more attracted to anyone in my life. On the other hand, there's a hardness about her. She used to be sweet."

"And she's not now?"

"That wasn't really the right word. I'll just say she was a lot more open and I didn't realize it before, but I kind of miss hearing about what's going on with her cats and what she saw on television the night before. All the rambling conversations I used to think annoyed me, I miss."

"Well, as the saying goes, you don't know what you've got until it's gone. So what do you two talk about now...or is there any use for words?"

Sebastian may have been thirty-six years old, but this was still his mother. His face grew hot and he didn't have to look into a mirror to know that he was beet red.

"Hmm, just as I thought. Honey, you really need to stop treating women like sex objects. I can't say I approve of your playboy ways. I hope you're being safe—you know, wearing protection," she finished on a whisper as if she'd just said a bad word.

"Mama!"

"What? I'm just making sure. I keep up with the news and realize there's a lot of nasty things floating out there. I know you're a grown man, but I want you to be careful. And try not to break her heart. That's the problem, isn't it? You're ready to end things, but you don't know how?"

"I wish that was it."

"Are you trying to say that you have feelings for this woman? Well, that's wonderful, isn't it?"

A huge lump formed in his throat and again his face grew warm, his ears burning. "She only wants sex."

A look of dismay crossed his mother's face. "What kind of woman is this? She doesn't sound like any girl I'd want for my precious baby to be with."

"Mama, these are different times from when you were growing up."

She rolled her eyes. "This women's lib stuff is a bunch of garbage, if you ask me. It's just an excuse for these young girls to be free and easy. Is this the kind of woman you want to be with?"

"Mama, please hear me out without passing judgment."

Pursing her lips, she folded her arms. "I'll try, son, but I don't like what I hear so far."

"We started seeing each other about a month ago, but things are stagnant. I want more, but she doesn't."

"Then get rid of her. A handsome guy like you can have any woman he wants."

A smile tilted the corner of his lips. "I hardly think so."

His mother crinkled her nose and he knew the cogs were spinning. "Do you really have feelings for her?"

"I don't know. I certainly feel something, but she won't let me find out what."

"I can't say I like the sound of this situation of yours, but if you want to find out, force her hand. Make it impossible for her to tell you no."

Sebastian hadn't thought of that before. He stroked his chin and mulled it over in his mind. "That just might work."

"Of course it will. Mama knows. Now, tell me about this woman of ill repute."

"Mama," he said in a warning tone.

"What?" She batted her eyes innocently. "I was just asking a question."

"You know what I'm talking about."

"Okay, okay. Your lady friend, what's her name?"

"Chastity."

His mother burst into loud laughter. "Talk about ironic."

"Please, Mama."

Wiping tears from her eyes, she stopped laughing. "I'm sorry, but you have to admit, that's pretty funny. Okay, tell me what Chastity is like."

"She's a paralegal and very bright. She has a superior grasp of her job. People usually go to her for the answers. And I've never heard her complain once. When I'm with her, I feel calm, yet I can't keep my hands to myself. She's very attractive. But the funny part is, months ago I didn't think so. I see glimpses of her kindness, and gentleness, but when I try to get closer, she shuts down."

"How do you mean?"

"If I ask personal questions, she either changes the subject or gives a flippant answer. I'm not sure how much more of this I can stand."

"Well, if you really feel she's worth this agony you're suffering, then you should take action. I'd certainly like to talk to this young lady and give her a piece of my mind for giving you the runaround like this. Even though you've probably had this coming for all the hearts you've broken in your lifetime, no one messes with one of my babies."

"In that case, I don't want to introduce her to you."

"I'd be on my best behavior."

Sebastian doubted that, but kept his opinion to himself. "There's something else."

"What? It can't be as bad as the other part."

"She's black."

His mother blinked a couple times, not saying a word. Sebastian knew she had her heart set on him settling down with a nice Italian girl, but there were just too many beautiful women in the world to narrow his view. He'd dated outside his race a handful of times, but since he'd never considered bringing any of his previous girlfriends home, it had never been an issue.

"Mama, say something."

"Well, this news does concern me a little. If you settle down with this woman, think of the hardships you'd face. Think about the children."

"Mama, I'll cross that bridge if it ever gets there, but if anyone has an issue about my being with Chastity, then that's their problem, not mine. I'd like to think I have your blessing if anything did come of this."

"Well, of course I'll support you in your choices, but you know how cruel the world is. Why make it harder on yourself than it has to be?"

"Is that what you really think?" he asked, slightly dismayed. His parents had not raised him to judge people based on the color of their skin, so hearing his mother talk this way was a surprise.

"Do you want me to pretty up my words and tell you that everything will be okay? I can't do that. I'm just trying to be honest with you. At the end of the day, the decision is yours and you're still my son. I love you, Sebastian, and if this woman is who you want to be with, I'll have to accept it. I'd rather gain a daughter than lose a son. I've seen it happen with a few of my friends."

"And that's unfortunate for them."

"I know. It would kill me to have a rift over something like this. The Cohans' daughter married a black guy and they sat Shiva for her. They act like she doesn't exist anymore, but I think it's sad. They're a couple of assholes anyway. Polly Cohan is probably better off without those two in her life. I don't want to lose you over something so trivial."

"You'll never lose me, Mama." Sebastian leaned over and pulled her into his embrace.

"You're such a good son, and I trust your judgment. If you want to be with this Chastity person, I could learn to love her."

Me too, he thought and that was the truly terrifying part.

ဆဝဆဝဆဝ

Chastity felt like she was being split in two. It was hard to keep pretending an indifference she didn't feel for Sebastian. In the beginning of this huge charade, she thought she'd be able to channel all her anger into the situation to carry on, but the more time she spent with him, the harder it became.

She saw a side of Sebastian she didn't know existed. When he wasn't taking her to the heights of passion, he let her in enough to see his true character. He'd always hold her after sex, stroking her hair while he shared tidbits of his life. She learned how his passion for law had come about, his hobbies, and goals. She saw the gleam of love and pride in his eyes when he talked about his family.

When he tried to find out things about her, however, Chastity wouldn't open up. That would mean trusting him and putting her heart on the line again. Maybe things would have been better if she'd never gotten this stupid makeover or better yet, if she'd never heard what he really thought of her. Then she wouldn't be struggling with these feelings.

Each time she was with him, she found herself falling just a little bit more for him. So what if he was attracted to her now? She'd seen enough of his women parading through the office to know his ardor wouldn't last. She wouldn't allow herself to be crushed by him again, so instead, she'd crush him.

Walking back to her condo, she scooped up Fluffy, who'd been waiting by the door. The walk she'd just taken hadn't cleared her mind. Actually, it had only given her more questions to think over. Taking a seat in her favorite chair, she stroked the purring cat absently behind the ear, wondering how she'd escape this mess unscathed. She started coughing violently.

Fluffy jumped off her lap and ran away. Chastity hoped she wasn't coming down with something. One of the reasons she took a walk in the first place was to shake off the lethargy she'd been feeling lately. Perhaps a cup of tea would make her feel better. As she stood, a wave of dizziness hit her, forcing her back down.

Making a second attempt to get up, she did it slowly this time, but still felt woozy. She walked to the kitchen on unsteady legs, and fixed her tea. When she took the mug out of the microwave, the phone rang. Chastity was tempted to ignore it, but Dallas had said she'd call this weekend to tell her about the new man she was seeing.

"Hello?"

"Chastity, honey, it's me, Brenda."

She wished she would have ignored the phone. Taking a deep breath she tried to inject as much enthusiasm into her voice as possible. "Hi. It's nice to hear from you. What's it been now? A couple months?"

"Well, you know how it is, dear. So many men, so little time. Well, maybe you don't, but I'm a busy woman. I do think about you though."

Her mother never failed to get in a little dig whenever she could. "I understand. So, how's life?"

"It's fabulous, as always. Uh, look, I'm going to be in your area next week, and I was hoping you'd give me a bed for a night."

"Of course you can stay with me."

"You know you'd have to put those filthy cats in the kennel while I'm there. I can't stand those nasty little beasts. And please be sure to give the place a good vacuuming, I don't want cat hairs on my clothes." Brenda sighed dramatically.

Chastity silently counted to ten before she spoke. "They're not filthy."

"But you will put them in a kennel or something before I come, right?"

"I'll make sure they're not around when you visit. So, what's the occasion? Will you be bringing Jared with you?"

"Oh, him. We broke up ages ago."

"You broke up with Jared? I thought he was the one."

"I thought so too, but there is that pesky little thing about him still being married. That bitch wife of his has threatened to cut him off if he doesn't stop seeing me."

"So he did?"

"Well, of course not. He knows he'll never find another woman like me. Jared only *told* her he'd stopped seeing me."

Chastity rolled her eyes. "So, why did you two break up then?"

"She tightened the purse strings anyway. I can't deal with that."

"So, you dumped him because he's not lavishing you with gifts anymore? That's kind of shallow."

"Sweetie, you're naïve. It's a man's world. A woman has to use what she has, to get what she wants. You'd have a man if you took that advice to heart."

It was on the tip of Chastity's tongue to tell her mother about Sebastian, but she decided against. The last thing she wanted was a running commentary on a situation she wasn't sure of herself. "Yes, I suppose so," she agreed meekly. "So, why are you coming up?"

"I'm driving through on my way to New York for a shopping excursion. I met this beautiful man online and he says we're going to paint the town."

"Brenda, you really should be careful. Will this be your first meeting?"

"Yes, but, we've talked on the phone almost every night. He sent me a present too, the most darling little necklace. It's only 18-karat gold, but it's a start. He's a stockbroker, living in a big empty house on Long Island."

Or an apartment in Bed Sty. "How do you know this guy is legitimate, and since when have you resorted to chatting online."

"Stop being an old fuddy-duddy. Jared bought me a computer so we could chat when he was home. We couldn't talk on the phone because the bitch listens in on his conversations and scans the cell phone bill every month."

"But instead of chatting with him, you used it to talk to other men?"

"He doesn't own me. Anyway, I don't see the harm in it."

"Only that you could potentially be meeting an ax murderer."

"Even if he does turn out to be an undesirable, I still have the credit card that's exclusively in Jared's name. I plan on using it to stay at the Waldorf Astoria. I'm meeting my hunk in the lobby, so we'll be on neutral ground. I'm not a complete airhead."

"Just be careful, okay? I hear so many bad things that could go wrong when you meet people online," Chastity cautioned.

Brenda laughed. "Don't be jealous, dear. Maybe you should look into internet dating. Some of the guys don't care what you look like."

Chastity was so used to those types of comments from her mother, that it didn't even faze her. Trying to talk sense into her mother was like trying to stop the sky from being blue. She sighed. "When exactly will you be here then?"

"This coming Friday. Well, I'd love to chat with you, but I have a date in an hour. Take care of yourself, honey." Brenda hung up before she could respond.

When Chastity replaced the phone on the hook, she slumped against the wall, feeling tired. Talking to her mother was always draining, but right now she felt positively weak.

Chapter Eleven

Sebastian navigated his way through downtown Philly traffic, breathing a sigh of relief when he pulled into the parking lot outside of his firm. Court had been hell this morning, waiting for a deliberation that could have gone either way. Fortunately the jury came back with the verdict he wanted.

He originally planned to go home and unwind, but the need to see Chastity drove him back to the office. Tonight he would take her out and wouldn't take no for an answer. Like his mother said, he'd have to force her hand and that's exactly what he intended to do. When he walked inside the building he nodded toward the receptionist.

"How are you today, Debbie?"

"Just great. How was court?"

"Grueling, but things turned out our way."

"Congratulations." She smiled at him before answering a call.

Sebastian walked past Chastity's desk on the way to his office only to find it empty. Maybe she was in the restroom. Shrugging, he went to his office to check messages. An hour later, he walked by her desk on the pretext of going to get a cup of coffee. She still wasn't there. Where the hell was she?

Just then, the object of his query came into his line of vision—no, it was more like wobbled. Something wasn't right. Her face, bare of make-up, had gray undertones. Dark circles rested under glazed eyes, and Chastity looked like she'd pass out at any second.

Hurrying to where she stood, he grabbed her arm. "Chastity, are you okay?"

"Yes, I'm fine."

Sebastian touched her cheek. She was hot. "You're not fine. You're burning up."

"She's been coughing and sneezing all morning, spreading her germs," Pearl broke in, spraying a can of aerosol disinfectant around her desk. Sebastian ignored her, focusing his attention on Chastity, who obviously wasn't well.

"I'm fine. I just need to sit down so the room can stop spinning."

"That's it. I'm taking you home. You're in no condition to get behind the wheel of a car."

"No. I'll call a friend."

"Kevin?"

She looked up at him with feverish eyes, but didn't confirm or deny. He could already guess the answer to that question and he'd be damned if he'd allow lover boy to get his hands on her. Ignoring her feeble protests, he helped Chastity collect her things. It briefly crossed his mind how things may have looked to the other workers, but he couldn't very well allow her to go home alone as she was now.

"Have a seat and I'll be back. I just have to let my secretary know I'm heading out again." He sat her down and she nodded, head drooping. After talking to his secretary, he caught Jeremy walking down the hall.

"Hey, Seb. I thought you weren't coming back in today."

"I, uh, had a couple things I needed to take care of first, but now I'm on my way out. Chastity is sick, so I'm taking her home."

Jeremy frowned. "She's sick? I've been holed up in my office all day. Is it serious?"

"Apparently she's been coughing and sneezing all day. I also think she may have a fever. It could be the spring flu."

"Do you think it's wise for you to take her home? This is how gossip gets started."

"She's sick. Any fool can see that."

"I'm just making an observation. Coupled with her makeover and all the times you find excuses to go by her desk, people will start to put two and two together. Look, I know this is none of my business, but even if you don't care about your own reputation, you should think about Chastity's."

Sebastian's eyes narrowed. "You're right. This is none of your business." He left Jeremy standing in the hallway. He knew his friend meant well, but making what was going on between him and Chastity seem sordid bugged the shit out of Sebastian.

He collected Chastity and led her to his car, under the watchful eyes of Pearl. He couldn't stand that woman. How anyone dealt with her was beyond him.

Chastity huddled close to the window, her head resting against the glass. "It's freezing in here," she whispered.

"Freezing? I don't have the air conditioner on." He reached over to touch her skin. She was still hot. Sebastian frowned. Chastity definitely needed to get some rest. "Do you have a lot of liquids at your house? You're going to need them, so you don't dehydrate."

"I haven't gone grocery shopping in a couple weeks. I meant to yesterday, but didn't feel up to it."

"That's it. We're going to my place."

She raised her head. "No, just take me home."

"Try to get some sleep."

"Sebastian, I'm serious. I'd like to go home to my own bed. Besides, I don't think I filled the cat dish for Monty and Fluffy this morning. They'll get hungry."

"I'm not going to take you home to an empty house and your cats don't count. Stop arguing and rest."

"But—"

"Chastity, I'm not going to continue this conversation. We're going to my house and that's that."

She gave him a resentful glare before leaning her head against the window again. "You always get what you want, don't you?"

"No. I don't actually."

She snorted with obvious disbelief, but didn't say anything else. Soon, her breathing became even as he drove to his Northeast Philly home. Not wanting to wake her when he pulled into his driveway, Sebastian carefully opened her door and lifted her out of the car.

His body tightened with awareness, the flowery scent of Chastity's perfume greeting his nostrils. It took some maneuvering for him to unlock his door and disarm the security system all while holding Chastity in his arms. To her credit, she didn't stir. When he laid her on the bed, his hands trembled, because he knew he'd need to undress her.

Rubbing his cock to ease the tormenting ache, he tried to get a hold of himself. There would be other times when he'd partake in her delectably lush body, but for now he needed to take care of her.

The last time he'd taken care of someone like this was when he still lived at home. His little sister, who'd been two at the time, had chicken pox, and his mother worked nights.

Forcing himself to keep his mind on the task at hand, he undressed her until she wore only panties. Sebastian tried not to let his gaze linger overly long on her large breasts that he enjoyed suckling while he fucked her. Unable to help himself, he gently ran his fingertip over one soft nipple, which instantly hardened.

Chastity moaned. He jerked his hand back, feeling like a pervert for touching her that way when she was too sick to do anything about it. He quickly tucked her underneath the covers. Just then, her eyes flickered open. "Sebastian," she whispered.

Sitting down next to her, he took her hand. "Yes, Chastity?"

"So cold."

"I know. Just snuggle under the blanket and get some rest. When you wake up, maybe you can try a little chicken broth."

"Not hungry."

"You're probably not hungry now, but maybe you will be when you wake up. How about trying to get some sleep?" He stroked her cheek, offering comfort the best way he knew how.

Her eyelids slowly drooped until she fell into a deep slumber. As he sat there watching her sleep, his heart thundered within his chest. The need to take care of her and just to be near her was stronger than he'd felt with anyone. When did this become more than just a wild affair to him? When did he start caring? How had she crept into his heart?

Was it when she revealed just how desirable she could be, or had it been before that, and he hadn't realized it? Whenever it was didn't matter. What did was finding out the extent of his feelings, and more importantly, Chastity's. Was this love? If he told her what was on his mind, would that push her away? Before her transformation, he would have been certain of her feelings for him, but sometimes she acted as though she didn't like him.

Chastity had him so confused. Sebastian didn't know how much longer his sanity would remain intact if things continued on as they were.

∞∞∞∞

Chastity slowly opened her eyes with her head pounding, throat raw, and the need to throw up. A warm swish of fur brushed against the side of her face, and she turned her head to see Fluffy resting by her side. It had all been a dream, yet it seemed so real.

Sebastian hadn't brought her to his house after all. But how did she get home? Her last coherent thought was of being at work, listening to Pearl harp on the fact that she'd brought germs into the office. Chastity groaned, trying to move her body.

"Ah, so you're finally awake. How are you feeling?" The smooth sound of Sebastian's voice filled the room. What was he doing in her bedroom? The bed depressed under his weight.

"What are you doing here?" she croaked, flinching when he placed a palm on her forehead.

"I live here."

Chastity licked painfully dry lips, focusing on her surroundings more clearly. What the hell? This wasn't her bed, nor was it her room. But what was Fluffy doing here? "I don't understand."

"You're sick, so I brought you home with me. While you've been sleeping, I went to your place and got some of your stuff. I even brought the wretched little fleabags you were so worried about."

"You brought Fluffy and Monty?" She knew he didn't care for her cats, so to hear that he'd done this for her was touching.

"Yes."

"But you hate them."

"And you love them. I didn't want to cause you unnecessary worry. And for my troubles, that damned Monty scratched me again."

Chastity would have laughed if she didn't ache. "It was nice of you to bring them here, but I'm quite capable of taking care of myself."

"If that were true, you wouldn't have gone to work in your current condition. And you'd have more in your refrigerator than a carton of Chinese food, milk and something in a container that's either spinach or the victim of an unfortunate experiment. Yeah, I've seen how well you take care of yourself."

"Why are you doing this, Sebastian?"

He gave her a long blank stare, but didn't answer. Instead, he switched the subject. "You're still really hot. Does your head hurt?"

Chastity wanted him to answer her question but was just too weak to pursue the topic. Maybe later. "Yes, it aches. I ache all over."

"I'll take you to the doctor in the morning to see if you can get some antibiotics. Are you up to eating a little something? I stopped by the grocery store and got a few things for you."

Just the thought of food made her stomach flip. "Ugh. No thanks. I'm just really tired. Maybe if I got a couple of aspirin for my head, I'll be fine. I don't want to be a bother."

"Lady, you have no idea what a bother you've been, but I've recently learned there's not a damn thing I can do about it."

If she didn't feel so miserable, Chastity would have asked him what he meant by that. She closed her eyes against the intensity of his green gaze.

"I'll get you those aspirins," he said softly, almost sounding disappointed. But why? And how in the world would she be able to walk away from him now, when he was showing yet another side of himself that was actually caring and sweet?

Sebastian was only gone for a short period of time before he returned with some tablets and a cup. "Come on, sit up a little." He helped her up.

When the covers shifted Chastity realized she was naked except for her underwear. "Did...did you undress me?"

"Your cats most certainly didn't. Stop trying to play the vestal virgin. I know your body intimately."

He put one pill against her lips before she could reply. She found it difficult to swallow with a sore throat. "Here, take a sip of this. It's ginger ale and should soothe your stomach a bit."

Once the arduous task of taking the pills, which felt like razors going down her throat, was done, Sebastian lowered her back down on the bed gently. She felt exhausted.

"Would you rather wear a nightshirt?" he asked.

"I'm dizzy enough from sitting up the first time. Besides, I think if I move again, I'm going to hurl."

"You poor baby," he murmured, sliding beside her, his arm resting lightly over her waist.

"Sebastian, what are you doing?" She tried to squirm away, risking nausea. He held her firm.

"Shh, just relax, and go to sleep."

But how can I, when you're holding me like this? And despite the fact that I'm sick, you're wreaking havoc on all my senses? As tired as Chastity was, she just wouldn't allow herself to relax. "Sebastian?"

"Hmm?"

"I appreciate you doing this for me, but..."

"But?"

"What about your workload? You have a life of your own to worry about, without me slowing you down."

"And what if I want to be slowed down?"

A smile tugged at the corners of her lips. "You almost sound like you mean it."

"I wouldn't have said it if I didn't mean it."

"You'll get sick."

"I'm never sick."

A weak chuckle erupted from Chastity's throat. "Famous last words."

"It's true. I think I got all the sickness out of my system during my childhood. When I was a baby, my parents didn't think I'd make it. My immune system wasn't very strong, and I was constantly getting colds, ear infections and any floating virus there was. Name it and I had it."

"You must have worried your mother to death."

"Probably, but I think I broke her in for my brother and sister. They didn't give her half as many gray hairs."

"So, just like that you stopped getting sick?"

"I think it was one of those freak things. When I was ten, I had the measles and I can honestly say that's probably the last time I've been sick. I haven't had so much as a cold."

"How is that possible?" she asked disbelievingly.

"Fast living?"

Chastity giggled, then winced. "Stop it. I'm not feeling up to laughing."

"So, go to sleep."

"I can't."

"Why not?"

"Because you're holding me too tight," she lied. The truth was, he wasn't holding her tight enough, but she'd be damned if she admitted it. Chastity was finding it exceedingly difficult to not care about him.

Sebastian released her, but he remained by her side. "I'm sorry. I just like holding you."

This was just too much. "Why, Sebastian?"

"Why what?"

"Why are you being so nice? I would have thought that by now you'd be tired of me. What's the record for you, anyway?"

He sat up abruptly, looking down at her with stormy eyes. "Where is this coming from?"

"It's coming from a place called common sense. You have to admit that you don't have the best track record with women."

"And how would you know about my love life?"

"I've seen the women come to the office and none of them lasted very long."

"None of those women were you."

She gasped. "Sebastian?"

"Forget I said that. You need the rest."

"Yes, I think I am rather tired," she said, wanting to change the subject as fast as he apparently did. Sebastian's heat of the moment confession was just the ammunition she needed to finally get her revenge, yet it gave her no joy.

Chapter Twelve

For the next four days, Sebastian waited on Chastity hand and foot, taking her to the doctor, picking up her prescriptions and forcing her to eat a little something. He also made sure she had clean linens every day. He even took good care of her cats.

Sebastian brought his work home so she wouldn't be alone. On Friday morning, Chastity felt refreshed except for a cough she couldn't quite shake. Otherwise, she was as good as new. She rolled over, seeking Sebastian's warmth. He wasn't there. Feeling bereft, she sat up. Even though she'd been sick, he'd slept with her every night, cradling her against his body. She'd found it comforting.

"Sebastian?" No answer.

She slid out of bed and nearly tripped over Monty. He growled at her before racing off. Chastity made her way downstairs. It was a large house for one man, but tastefully decorated. Yesterday was the first day he'd allowed her out of bed and he'd showed her around. The funny thing was, she could see herself in this place, permanently.

That's when Chastity knew she'd have to go home, and fast. If she stayed here any longer, she'd never want to leave. The smell of bacon and fresh coffee permeated the air and led to the kitchen. She found Sebastian in front of the stove, wearing an apron and a pair of snug jeans that hugged his tight ass.

A pool of moisture formed in her panties. *Get a hold of yourself, girl.* She should have been at the point where the sight of him didn't make her pulse race the way it did.

"Good morning, Chastity," he greeted, without turning around. He'd obviously spotted her in the mirror above the stove.

"Good morning," she said, tentatively stepping into the kitchen and taking a seat.

"I'm glad you're up. You're just in time for breakfast. How do you like your eggs?"

"I don't really have much of an appetite right now."

"But you have to eat something. You haven't eaten a lot all week, and if you want your strength back, you need to get something substantial in your belly."

She knew better than to argue with him. "Fine. If I have to eat, how about a slice of toast and some coffee?"

"I think I can do better than that. I'll put some scrambled eggs and bacon on your plate. Just take a few bites for me."

"Okay, but I'm not going to finish it all."

"Just as long as you give it a try, is all I ask."

"I didn't know you cooked."

"When you're the oldest sibling, and your mother has to work two jobs to make ends meet, sometimes you have to be in charge of the household stuff like cooking and cleaning."

"Wow. You're a regular jack-of-all-trades. You're a brilliant attorney, you cook and you're a great caretaker. Cute apron, by the way."

He turned around with a wide grin on his face. The words read: kiss the cook. "So, you like this, do you?"

"I must admit that you look...interesting in it."

"Not sexy?" he teased.

"Maybe a little."

His grin widened. "I guess I'll have to wear this more often then." He placed a plate in front of her.

Chastity's eyes widened at the amount of food he'd heaped on it. "Sebastian, there's no way I'll be able to finish all of this." With wary eyes, she surveyed the meal before her of toast, bacon, eggs and a grapefruit half.

"Just eat a little."

With a sigh, she picked up her fork. After a few bites, Chastity discovered that she was indeed hungry. She stopped shoveling food into her mouth long enough to shoot Sebastian a sheepish grin when he sat down with his own plate.

"Not hungry, huh?"

"Okay, I guess I was hungrier than I thought."

"Now that you're up, I was thinking that I could take you out of the house today."

In the middle of taking a bite of bacon, she pushed her plate away. Now was the time to tell him or she'd never get it off her chest. "About that. I'm feeling so much better and I think I should go back home today. I'd like it if you would take me to the office, so I can get my car."

"There's no hurry. You're not going to work today, and tomorrow's Saturday."

Chastity smacked her forehead, remembering that her mother was supposed to visit today. At least now, she had a legitimate excuse without causing an argument. "I have to go home. My mother is coming today. I completely forgot."

His green eyes narrowed, studying her face. "Is this the truth or just another excuse not to spend time with me? This is getting really old, Chastity."

"I'm telling the truth. My mother is really coming today. The thing is, she didn't tell me what time she'd be arriving. Knowing her, it probably won't be until later, but I have to clean my place up for her."

"Why is this the first time I'm hearing about this?"

"Gee, Sebastian, I didn't realize I had to report every detail of my life to you."

His mouth tightened, nostrils slightly flaring. "Fine. I'll go with you. I'd love to meet your mother."

The last thing she needed was to see Brenda clinging to Sebastian like a limpet. "I don't think so. I only see her once in a blue moon, so you understand, don't you?"

"I didn't say I'd stick around, just that I'd like to meet her."

"Why?"

"Because she's your mother. Why not?"

"You know what I mean. Why are you acting as if we're in a relationship? We're not, you know."

"Maybe I'd like to be."

He had to be kidding. Chastity laughed. "I think you may be the one coming down with something. Is your head warm?"

"I mean it, Chastity," he said quietly.

Sebastian was serious. She stopped laughing. Was this it? Could she drop the bomb on him now? Something held her back. "Sebastian, this wasn't what we agreed on."

"I don't think we've agreed on anything. You've been holding me at arm's length since we began this thing and I don't like it one bit."

"We're just fucking, that's all. Why do you have to make things more complicated than they already are?"

"Just fucking?" he asked, his voice dangerously quiet.

Chastity shrugged, trying to maintain her air of nonchalance. "I haven't relegated this to anything. It is what it is and I'm just trying to be honest. If you really thought about it, you'd probably realize what a favor I'm doing for you."

"And what favor might that be?" he asked tightly, his eyes shooting green fire.

"No strings attached sex. Isn't that what every man wants? Besides, why rock the boat? If it's not broke, don't fix it, right?"

Sebastian's eyes narrowed and his lips tightened to a thin, angry line. "Is this what you want? No strings attached sex?"

No! Chastity wanted to scream and shout that she wanted more too, but fear held her tongue steady. She wouldn't let him hurt her again. "Of course it's what I want. Haven't I already said so?"

Sebastian's nostrils flared. "How are you feeling right now?"

"Fine. Good enough to go home."

Sebastian pushed his plate away and stood up. Striding over to where she sat, he grabbed her wrist.

"What are you doing?" Chastity tried to force herself from his grasp, but it was iron-clad.

"You said you were better, so how about some of that no strings attached sex you're so fond of."

Shaking her head vigorously, Chastity trembled. "No. I'm not in the mood."

"But I am, and you don't get to call all the shots." Yanking her out of her seat, Sebastian pulled Chastity into his arms. He covered her mouth with a hungry, brutal kiss. When she tried to turn her head away, Sebastian grabbed a fistful of hair, forcing her head straight.

"No," she whispered against his mouth, even though her traitorous body started to melt against his. Chastity's nipples grew into tight points as they strained against his chest.

"Open your mouth, goddammit," he muttered against her lips, tugging on her hair. When she gasped at his forcefulness, Sebastian's tongue shot into her mouth, aggressively. Pulses of sensation shot through her nervous system, her arms inching themselves around his narrow waist.

Releasing her hair, Sebastian slid his hand down her back and cupped her bottom, squeezing and kneading it, molding her body closer to his. Sebastian's cock pressed against her thigh, and her legs went weak.

Sebastian held her firm, his mouth still ruthlessly claiming hers. She was a fool to think she'd be able to break things off so easily, especially when Sebastian only had to give her one look in order for her body to burst into flames. Drowning in a sea of passion, Chastity wasn't sure that she wanted to be rescued.

Anger may have driven him to pull her in his arms, but it was lust that kept her there. No other woman had ever made him feel the need to strangle and screw her at he same time. He'd taken care of her all week and in his own way, tried to show her that he did indeed have feelings for her, only to have his deed tossed back in his face. So she wanted to fuck? Then he'd give her what she wanted.

Lifting his head, Sebastian pushed Chastity against the kitchen table and yanked off the tablecloth, sending everything crashing to the floor. "Sebastian!" she gasped in horror. "What are you doing?"

"I'm not doing anything yet, but I fully intend to fuck you."

She placed quivering hands against his chest, her eyes wide with an unreadable emotion, yet Chastity didn't push him away. "Not like this, Sebastian," she whispered weakly.

"Yes, like this. It's what you wanted, right? You just want to be fuck buddies."

"But I—"

"Changed your mind?" he growled. "Well that's just too damn bad, because this is exactly what you asked for and you're going to get it." He pushed her on the table and tore her nightshirt down the front, baring generous globes. She turned her head to the side, as if she couldn't look at him, but not before he saw the gleam of desire in her eyes.

He trailed a fingertip over one taut peak, making her tremble. "Don't pretend like you don't want this, Chastity, because your body will always give you away."

"Please," she whispered.

"Oh, don't worry about that, baby. I intend to." Sebastian placed one hand against her belly while slowly sliding the other one up her thigh. Then he pushed her legs apart and rubbed Chastity's cunt through her underwear.

He chuckled. "You see? I've barely touched you and you're already wet. You hunger for my cock, don't you? You can't get enough of it."

"You're a son of a bitch," she muttered, raising her chin defiantly.

"But you want this son of a bitch, don't you? What does that make you?" Pushing the crotch of her panties aside, he spread her labia with two fingers, pushing into her pussy.

"Oh!" she exclaimed, squirming as he slid his fingers out then jammed them back into her wet hole.

"Does this pussy get wet like this for your friend Kevin?"

"There's nothing between Kevin and I. He's just—"

"Just a friend? Oh, yeah, I've heard that line before." He finger fucked her until all Chastity could do was whimper and moan.

Her eyes lit up with lust and wonder as she orgasmed, her juices flowed over his hand as he rubbed her tight anal ring with two fingers. Sebastian enjoyed pushing his cock into her hot cunt more than anything else, but the delight of thrusting into her big round bottom was a treat he couldn't pass up.

Chastity, he'd discovered, loved his cock in her ass. There were nights when he'd slide his come-soaked dick past that puckered hole and she'd scream as if she couldn't get enough. He wanted to hear that scream now. Wounded pride would not allow him to settle for less than her absolute surrender.

He unfastened his pants and eased his cock out. Jesus, he was hard. She looked so beautifully wanton, laying on the kitchen table, breasts heaving, and a look of unabashed desire. "Do you know what I'm going to do to you now, Chastity?" he asked, pulling her panties completely off before slipping another damp finger into her butt.

"You're going to stick your cock into my rear," she groaned, gyrating her hips against his hand.

"That's right, baby, but first I'm going to make you beg for it."

"And if I don't?" she whispered back, nearly breathless.

"Then I'll stop." It was a lie, but she didn't know that. Walking away when he was so fucking hard would have been like cutting his own arm off.

"You wouldn't," Chastity shrewdly challenged.

Sebastian halted the back and forth motion of his fingers. "Try me. As much as I enjoy fucking this juicy pussy and ass, I can easily go to the bathroom and finish this myself. What would you do?"

"I'll...I can do the same. I don't need you."

Sebastian threw his head back and laughed. "Keep telling yourself that, sweetheart. We both know it won't be as good as the real thing. Go ahead. Walk away. I dare you."

Chastity lay there, her mouth opening and closing. As she nibbled on her bottom lip, Sebastian nearly lost it. Damn, why didn't she say anything?

With downcast eyes, she whispered, "You know I can't walk away. Please, finish what you started." She wiggled her ass against his hand, obviously wanting him to continue.

Sebastian hadn't realized he'd been holding his breath, until he exhaled deeply. Chastity was so unpredictable at times, he didn't know what would come out of her mouth, but he'd have his payback. "Beg for it."

Her lips tightened momentarily, but when he started to move his finger in and out of her anus again, she released a ragged sigh. "Fuck my ass, Sebastian. Please fuck me now! I need you. I beg of you. There! Is this what you wanted to hear?"

"Yes. That's exactly what I wanted to hear." Slowly he pulled his fingers out of her ass, and then grasped his cock. "Spread your cheeks. Offer yourself to me, Chastity."

Trembling hands cupped her rounded bottom, as she obeyed his command. Sebastian's breath caught in his throat at the erotic sight before him. Her dark labia opened ever so slightly to reveal the tempting pinkness within. Come oozed to the crack of her ass. She'd be plenty wet for him.

Sebastian licked his lips. "What a delicious sight you make, Chastity. There's nothing more beautiful than you on your back open, ready and wet for my cock. When I enter you, I want you to say my name."

"Anything you want, just do it."

It suddenly dawned on him that he wasn't wearing a condom. "Shit," he cursed, not wanting this moment to end.

Chastity frowned. "What's the matter?"

"I don't have protection."

She stiffened, before a smile crossed her face. "We've discussed our sexual histories with each other. We're both in good health, and I'm on the pill. Besides, I want to feel your skin against mine."

A sensation of pure ecstasy raced down his spine. There was nothing he wanted more right now, than to fuck her without the barrier of a rubber. The intimacy of it was something he'd only shared with one other woman, and that had been a foolish moment in college that had him nervously waiting in a clinic weeks later. Fortunately, he'd been given a clean bill of health, but Sebastian vowed he'd never be that careless again. With Chastity, however, things were different. "Are you sure?"

"Very sure."

Pushing the tip of his dick against her anus, he slid it along her crack. She moaned. "Stop teasing me and stick it in."

"How badly do you want it?"

"Very badly. Do it now!" she screamed, the frustration evident in her voice.

Sebastian chuckled, before sliding past the puckered ring. He moaned as he slid deeper into her tight rectum. It was so snug and wet, he felt like he'd explode right then and there. He watched her expression while he pushed inch by inch of his cock into her ass.

Chastity shouted. "Sebastian! Sebastian! Sebastian! Fuck my ass!" She wiggled beneath him.

His hands dug into her hips as he pounded into her, his balls slapping against the seat of her ass, making it jiggle. Leaning forward, he nipped Chastity on the side of her neck, the primitive need to brand her taking hold of him. This was his ass and pussy and he wanted Chastity to know it as well.

"Finger your clit for me," he ordered huskily.

She rubbed two fingers between her swollen cunt lips, squirming and moaning. "Sebastian, I'm going to come."

"Then do it. Don't hold back."

Chastity's thighs quivered, the movement slowly taking over her entire body. "Sebastian! Oh my God!"

A warm stream of honey flowed from her cunt and oozed down her crack. His cock was slicker than ever. His own orgasm was near. Pounding into her luscious backside as hard as he could, he shot his seed up her rectum. "This ass belongs to me and only me."

"Yes! It's yours!" she cried, pulling him against her, their mouths melding together.

The table, not built to take their collective weight, began to wobble. "Damn, I have to get up before this thing collapses under us," he sighed. No sooner had the words left his mouth, did the table give way, sending them crashing to the floor.

Chastity broke Sebastian's fall. Her hands flew to her face and her shoulders started to shake. Alarm seized him. He'd hurt her. Sebastian eased his cock out of her ass, his come seeping out. "Chastity, are you okay? Honey, speak to me." Her shoulders shook even harder. "Baby, tell me where it hurts. Please, don't cry."

She took her hands off her face and to his surprise she was laughing. "Chastity, I thought you were hurt."

She laughed louder than ever. "I'm sorry, but that was pretty funny. I guess you're going to have to get a new kitchen table." She wiped a tear from her eye. Now that he knew Chastity was okay, he also saw the humor in the situation. Sebastian had seen plenty of movies where people had had sex on the kitchen or dining room table, but none of the scenes ever ended quite like this.

Pulling her close, he stroked Chastity's back, wishing the moment would never end, but he knew it would have to. Just how could he convince her that what they had was more than just sex?

Chapter Thirteen

"I can't thank you enough for taking care of me and sending your housekeeper over to clean my place. I owe you so much," Chastity sighed. When she'd checked her answering machine from Sebastian's place there'd been a message from her mother, who said she'd be in town around seven, which gave them plenty of time to get her house ready.

"It's my pleasure."

"And you don't mind keeping Fluffy and Monty with you? I know how much you dislike them, but I—"

He covered her lips with one finger. "Chastity, it's okay. I don't mind doing this for you."

And that was exactly what worried her. What was Sebastian up to? First, he'd taken care of her. She supposed she could have objected, but that would only have ended with her getting thoroughly fucked.

"I accept your thanks. Look, I should get going since you want some alone time with your mother."

She lowered her lids, trying to hide her anxiety.

"What?"

"What what?"

"What was that look for? I thought you wanted me to go, although I'd much rather stay."

"Seeing my mother always makes me nervous."

"Why?"

"We don't really have a typical mother-daughter relationship. I don't want you to think that my reluctance for you to meet her is because of you."

"I see. Well, unless you hide me in your bedroom, I don't think there's any avoiding that now."

She frowned, her forehead creasing. "What do you mean?"

"Is that her coming up your driveway?"

"Oh, crap," she muttered. With a shrug, Chastity released a deep sigh. "Well, I guess you'll get your wish after all."

"Is it really going to be so bad?" he asked gently.

"You'll find out soon enough for yourself." An impending sense of dread washed over her. When the doorbell rang, Chastity took a deep breath and answered.

Instead of a hello or long time no see, Brenda's eyes widened. "What happened to you?" The question came out as though it was an unpleasant surprise to see her daughter's transformation.

There wasn't much that had changed about her mother however. Still slender as ever, Brenda's caramel skin glowed without the hint of a wrinkle, belying her forty-six years, although she'd only admit to forty of those years. Her perfectly coiffed hair rested on her shoulders, and make-up expertly done. She reminded Chastity of a younger, sexier version of Diane Carroll.

"How was your trip?" Chastity ignored Brenda's question, opening her door wider to let her mother in.

Brenda frowned. "Are those cats around?"

"No, they're at a friend's."

When Brenda's hazel gaze locked on Sebastian, a faint look of surprise entered her eyes before a wide smile split her face. "Well, hello. Don't tell me you're one of Chastity's friends." She held out her hand as though she expected him to kiss it.

Chastity rolled her eyes. *Here we go.*

Sebastian shook the hand offered to him, but immediately let it go much to Brenda's obvious displeasure. "Sebastian Rossi. I'm very pleased to meet you, ma'am."

"Ma'am!" came Brenda's outraged squawk. "Bite your tongue, Sebastian. I'm much too young to be called ma'am. I was practically a baby when I had Chastity. People mistake us for sisters, and most of the time they think I'm the younger one, but my daughter has always been a bit of an old soul."

Chastity balled her fists at her side. Her mother was bearable and actually fun to be with when there wasn't a man around. "How about I put your things in the room you'll be sleeping in tonight. Would you like something to drink?" Chastity asked as a means to escape the now stifled room.

"Diet soda...if you have it. I'm trying to maintain my girlish figure. It really wouldn't hurt if you put forth the effort either, dear." The barb hit its mark, making Chastity's face grow hot with embarrassment. Seeming satisfied that she'd gotten her point across, Brenda then turned to her prey. "Now, Sebastian, tell me what you do for a living," the older woman cooed, smiling at him like the Cheshire cat.

Humiliation and anger burned in Chastity's stomach. Not waiting to hear Sebastian's response, she left the room to put her mother's things in the bedroom before storming to the kitchen. She knew this would happen the moment her mother laid eyes on Sebastian. No matter what the circumstances, the woman just wouldn't stop competing.

He was probably eating it up, just like the other men Brenda set out to charm, so it was a surprise to find him pacing the floor, a perturbed expression on his face when she returned.

"Here's your soda, Brenda. I hope diet cola is okay."

"Thank you, honey. Sebastian and I were having the most delightful conversation. You didn't tell me he was your boss, Chastity. I guess that explains why he's here."

Chastity didn't have to ask her mother what that meant because she already knew. Normally, Brenda's cattiness just rolled off her back, but with Sebastian standing witness, the comments stung.

"And exactly why would you think I'm here?" Sebastian asked, turning his quizzical green gaze her mother's way.

"You're obviously here to work. Chastity is always willing to go that extra mile. She was like that in school as well, doing extra credit work—you know, always the teacher's pet. But, I guess since she didn't have much of a social life, she didn't have anything better to do."

"Brenda, I doubt Sebastian wants to hear anymore about my high school years," Chastity said through clenched teeth, her face burning with shame.

"On the contrary. I'd love to hear more," Sebastian said, taking a seat next to Brenda.

The older woman beamed triumphantly, sending her daughter a smug look as she touched Sebastian on the knee. "I have so many stories to tell. I don't know where to start," Brenda trilled.

Chastity took a seat, with the feeling of her heart being squeezed. If she could just imagine she was somewhere else right now, this wouldn't be so bad.

Sebastian prodded. "I'm sure you can think of something." Why was he doing this to her? Had he fallen under her mother's spell too? Brenda was a man-eater and if Sebastian couldn't see through it, then they were welcome to each other.

"Well, you really can't say she's had the most exciting life. I guess she takes after her father, God rest his soul. He had a lot of meat on his bones too, but it looks so much more attractive on a man." Brenda's eyes cut slyly in Chastity's direction, and it took everything within her not to get up and walk out of the room.

She should have known that nothing much had changed where her mother was concerned, but Chastity hadn't counted on someone witnessing it.

"I will have to disagree with you there. I think a little extra 'meat' as you so delightfully put it, looks rather well on some women. And maybe I'm a little biased where Chastity is concerned, but I think she carries herself rather well."

Chastity didn't know whether to laugh at the comical look on Brenda's face, who clearly wasn't used to being gainsaid, or to smile at Sebastian's defense of her.

Again her mother laughed, this time sounding phonier than ever. "You're such a sweet man, Sebastian, for being so kind to Chastity. I am, of course, glad to see that she's not a total disaster now. Lord knows she's spent most of her life in the awkward stage. I guess she inherited some of my genes after all." Brenda sighed like the long-suffering matron.

"She certainly didn't inherit her personality from you. On my short observation, you two are night and day," he intimated.

"Oh, heavens no. I'm much more outgoing. I guess that's why all of her little friends used to gravitate toward me, whenever she brought them home."

Sebastian looked Chastity's way, but she refused to meet his eyes. She felt like screaming and telling her mother to stop running her down, but once again, the old insecurities took over. She looked down at her lap, her hands tightly clenched together.

"Can I ask you something, Brenda?" he asked, his voice dropping an octave.

"Of course, sweetheart. You can ask me anything."

"Great, because I'd really like to know why you feel the need to rip your daughter apart the way you do. You just met me, yet you've let me know just how little you think of her. She's sat there and taken it like a lady, when most women would have knocked you out by now. You claim to have the looks and personality between the two of you, but it's obvious to me who got the class."

Brenda's mouth fell open, giving her the appearance of a gaping fish. She wasn't the only one left speechless because Chastity was floored. Chastity couldn't remember a time when anyone, let alone a male, had ever talked to her mother like that.

Brenda took a moment to recover. Blinking, she said, "I beg your pardon?"

"You heard me. If you haven't figured it out yet, Chastity and I are more than just employer and employee. I care about her very much and take exception to anyone talking about her in the way you have for the past twenty minutes."

Brenda shot Chastity a pleading look. "Are you going to allow him to talk to me like that, Chastity?"

"Uh, Sebastian, I think it's probably best if you left. I appreciate everything you've done for me this week, but I need to spend some alone time with my mother."

His mouth tightened. "Is that what you really want?"

She nodded. "I think it's for the best. Let me walk you to your car."

Once they were outside, Sebastian let loose. "How could you just sit there and let her do that to you?"

"She's been doing it all my life. I'm used to it now. Most times, she's really not like she was just now."

"There was a lot more I would like to have told her, but I had to keep in mind that she's your mother. It's too bad she's forgotten that."

Chastity was touched by his indignation on her behalf. She placed her hand against his broad chest, stood on the tip of her toes and gave him a kiss on his jaw. "Thank you. No one has ever stood up for me like that before."

"Then why are you asking me to leave? Her picking will probably get worse without me around."

"No. It will get better. She only gets that way when there are men around, and no matter what, she's still my mother. We don't have a made-for-television kind of relationship, but I understand her."

"Then make me understand too, because I wanted to shake her."

Chastity's heart did a series of somersaults. It was going to be hard as hell walking away from the way he made her feel. Her conscience told her to sever ties now to make the break easier, but as she looked into his pale green eyes, Chastity couldn't do it.

"From an early age, my mother had been told how beautiful she is. She grew up in a situation where her mind wasn't nurtured. All she had was her looks to rely on. As she gets older, Brenda realizes her own mortality. How can I hold it against her, when I know just how insecure she is? I admit that sometimes what she says can be hurtful and makes me doubt myself, but I've learned to accept her for the person she is."

Sebastian cupped her cheek, his thumb moving lightly over her skin. "You're amazing, Chastity. I only wish—you're very wise to see that."

She smiled at his compliment although it didn't distract her from the fact that he'd changed what he'd really wanted to say in midstream. She wondered what it was, but decided not to delve further into the matter. "A good friend pointed it out to me not very long ago. In her own way, she does care about me, but I've learned the hard lesson that the only approval I need is mine."

He brushed his lips against hers, causing a stirring between her thighs. "When shall I bring your wretched animals back?"

"Brenda is heading out in the morning."

"Good. I'll bring them back at noon. We'll make a day of it." Chastity would have protested, but Sebastian covered her lips with his finger. "I won't take no for an answer. See you tomorrow?"

She nodded, against her better judgment. Sebastian gave her another quick kiss before walking to his car. It just wasn't right for one man to look so damn sexy. When his car drove out of her line of vision, she sighed in resignation and walked back into her house, only to find her mother looking more than slightly miffed.

"Sorry that took so long," Chastity apologized.

"Who does that man think he is? Did you hear him call me classless? I hope you gave him the what for."

Here we go again. "Uh, yeah. We did have a talk, but you know, Brenda, you were laying it on a bit thick."

Hazel eyes widened, the picture of mock innocence. "What did I do? He asked about you and I told him."

"Yes, but it's funny that you always manage to come out on top at my expense."

"What are you trying to say?"

"Absolutely nothing. If I thought it would make a difference, I'd have plenty to say, but it's probably better if we just drop it."

"No. I don't want to drop it. Chastity, I may not be the best example of motherhood, but I do love you. If something I've said or done has upset you, I wish you'd let me know."

"Brenda, it's much too late to play the mother role with me."

The older woman released a sigh, twisting the large emerald ring on her finger. "You're right. I haven't been a very good parent to you, but I did the best I could. Maybe I can never be the maternal figure you need, but can't we at least be friends?"

Chastity shrugged. "That's the problem. I never wanted your friendship. I wanted a mother. I'd like to be able to have a conversation with you without being told what a loser I am."

Brenda frowned. "I don't think you're a loser."

"Really? It sure seems like you do. Look, I realized that it's not me. It's just the way you are, but sometimes, like today, you can be extremely hurtful. I've had enough."

"I see." Brenda stood and walked over to her daughter. "Sweetheart, I don't ever think I can be the person you want me to be, but I'm sorry that I've hurt you. I...well, the truth is, I've just been so damn jealous of you. I hated myself sometimes and instead of—" She broke off to nibble on her bottom lip.

Chastity was too stunned to hear her mother admit what others had only speculated. It was obviously a day of revelations. "Jealous of me? You're gorgeous, and men fall over themselves to get to you."

A faint smile touched Brenda's burgundy-smeared lips. "There's no denying that, but so are you, sweetheart. You look great, by the way. I knew you always had so much potential, and that's why...I'm not proud to admit this, but I flirted with all your boyfriends to prove to myself that I was still a desirable woman. Call me ignorant, but I didn't realize how damaging that was to you. I was too wrapped up in my own self and issues to see that you were hurting. Besides, men look at me and want one thing. Men look at you and they want more."

"Hardly," Chastity snorted. "I was such an introvert."

"Yet, you inspire loyalty in a lot of people. Look at how protective Dallas is of you, and you remember that silly boy you brought home from school and caught me with? While he was with me, all he could do was talk about you. He was guilty as hell afterwards and I really think he cared about you, but you know how boys think with their little heads at that age."

This was news to Chastity.

"And look at your Sebastian...if I were you, girl, I'd hold on to that man and never let go. It's obvious he's crazy about you, Chastity. I've never said this before, but I'm very proud of you and I admire you."

Hearing her mother say the words after all this time meant a lot. Brenda wrapped her slender arms around Chastity and kissed her on the cheek. It was the first time Chastity's mother had ever hugged her since she was very small. Maybe things would be okay between the two of them now.

Chastity didn't fool herself into thinking that things would be perfect, but at least an understanding had been reached. Now, all she had to do was figure out what she should do about Sebastian.

Chapter Fourteen

Chastity pushed away from her desk and stood to stretch her tense muscles. She must have been sitting for three hours straight, the last half hour of which she'd spend trying to draft the same letter. A nice massage would be great right now, she thought, but it wouldn't solve her problems.

If anything, work was the least of her worries. Things weren't going according to plan. In fact, her mission to exact revenge against Sebastian Rossi had gone completely haywire. When she and her friends had come up with their strategy, Chastity didn't calculate on falling even harder for him than she had before. A few months had now passed since they'd become lovers, and each time they came together was explosive.

Chastity would daydream about the way his tongue danced over her body, how his cock felt plundering her wet pussy, and the way he'd hold her afterwards, stroking and kissing her neck as if they were more than just fuck buddies.

The thing was, she wasn't really sure what they were anymore. From the day he'd taken her to his house to take care of her, there'd been a shift in control. Sebastian no longer allowed her to call all the shots. They'd fallen into a pattern. At work, things were kept as professional as possible, with the exception of the time he'd caught her in the file room alone.

Sebastian had quickly locked the door, pulled her against his hard body and fingered her until her knees went weak. Most nights when he wasn't bogged down with work, Sebastian would come to her place or she'd go to his and they'd fuck until all hours of the night. On the weekends, they'd go out, doing things like a real couple. Even her friends were beginning to suspect there was something going on between the two of them that had nothing to do with Chastity seeking revenge.

She shouldn't have let things go this far, and now Sebastian was talking about taking her to Long Island to meet his mother. Chastity glanced at her desk clock and sighed. Five o' clock, quitting time, yet there was still so much to be done. Sebastian had made no mention of getting together tonight, since he didn't know what time he'd get back from court.

Maybe that was for the best. It would give her time to figure out what she needed to do. Whatever it was, Chastity had to do it fast, or else she would be in deeper than she already was. Even though she had a pile of paperwork on her desk, she figured it wasn't anything that couldn't wait until tomorrow. Just as she was shutting down her computer, Sebastian walked over, startling her. "Chastity."

She jumped in surprise. "Holy cow, Sebastian! You're going to give me a heart attack."

"I'm sorry. I know this is short notice, but do you mind staying late tonight? I have a few things I'm going to need to have done by tomorrow morning."

Chastity furrowed her brows. He looked distracted, cagey almost, as if something was weighing heavily on his mind. "Sure. What do you need me to do?" she asked, grabbing her pad and pen. In this way she could relate to him, because then she didn't have to analyze her feelings. She jotted down a list of items he rattled off to her.

"Anything else?" she asked.

"No. I think that's it. If you need me, I'll be in my office. I'm staying late as well." There was no sexual undertone to this statement, which was fine, but again, Chastity got the impression that there was something going on that he wasn't letting on to.

"Okay. I got it."

"Oh, and don't worry. A few others have agreed to help out as well. I really appreciate you doing this for me."

Pearl chose that moment to walk over to them, hands on hips and lips pursed in one thin, angry line. Her faded blue eyes narrowed slightly as she looked up at Sebastian. "Don't expect me to stay late. Carl and I have our bowling league tonight. You can't expect a body to stay late without giving proper notice."

Chastity wanted to sock the old biddy. In the last several weeks, Pearl had become harder to deal with, constantly muttering under her breath and making snide comments. On most days, Chastity could ignore her, but there were times, like today, when the urge to shake the disagreeable woman was nearly too strong to resist.

"Sebastian was talking to me, Pearl, not you," Chastity pointed out.

Pearl's head whipped around so fast she looked like the kid on the Exorcist. Her eyes shooting daggers. "I wasn't talking to you, Miss High and Mighty. Just because the two of you are having an affair, doesn't give you the right to talk to me like your stuff doesn't stink."

It was now Sebastian's turn to glare. Lifting a sinister dark brow, he asked, "I beg your pardon? Would you care to repeat that, Pearl?"

Embarrassment flickered briefly over the older woman's face, before defiance replaced it. "Well, it's no big secret that the two of you have something going on. I see the way you look at each other, and personally, I think it's disgusting. You two have made this a hostile work environment for a decent Christian woman like me."

"Those are very serious charges you're levying against us. Have you caught the two of us in the act?"

Pearl's nostrils flared. "I'm not stupid. I don't have to see it, to know it's happening! I see the way you two go off together. Aren't there rules against stuff like this?"

Sebastian remained expressionless, but Chastity could tell he was pissed. "I suggest you think long and hard before you bring this up again in my or Chastity's presence, if you want to continue working here." He spoke with such dead calm that made Chastity feel the chill from where she stood.

Pearl lost all color in her face. Chastity couldn't figure out if Pearl was incredibly stubborn or just plain stupid when she didn't back down right then and there. "Oh, so now you're threatening me for speaking my mind? I work just as hard as the African Queen over here, but because I don't spread my legs for you, I'm the one who gets the flack."

Chastity's hand flew to her mouth to hide her gasp. Pearl had said some pretty nasty things in the past, but nothing this vicious. She was practically begging to be fired. Instead of exploding like Chastity thought he would, Sebastian remained calm.

"That's quite enough, Pearl. No one is keeping you here right now. Have fun at your bowling league tonight, but I think you should start looking for a position elsewhere, if you have a problem working in this 'hostile environment'. As a matter of fact, it would probably be for the best," he said, before turning to Chastity. "Thanks for staying." He walked off then.

Chastity shook her head at Pearl, who stood there with her mouth agape. "You miserable old battle-ax. Sebastian has more class in his pinky than you have in your entire body."

"How sweet of you to defend your lover, but he'll soon get tired of you like the rest of the sluts who parade through here. His kind can't keep it in his pants. I can't wait to find another job and get away from the likes of you two."

"Pearl, you're going to make me forget I'm a lady, and that you're old enough to be my grandmother, if you don't leave this minute."

"I'll leave when I'm good and ready. I'm not going to let some stupid cow tell me what to do. You're nothing but a dumb—"

"Say it, and I'll hand your teeth back to you in a bag." Chastity's hands clenched into tight fists. Pearl must have read something in her eyes because she quickly turned away muttering under her breath.

Chastity stood with folded arms as she watched her nemesis gather her things. Pearl sent her one last scathing look before marching off in a huff. Old bitch. With a deep breath, Chastity sat down at her desk again. It wasn't the first time someone had insulted her, and unfortunately it wouldn't be the last, but she was still ticked.

She plopped on her headphones, slipped in James Taylor's greatest hits CD and began tackling the list that Sebastian had given her. Several CD's later and a huge dent in her list, Chastity glanced at the clock. Seven-thirty. Removing headphones, she stood and stretched, her stomach starting to rumble.

She walked to co-workers' desks to see if there were any dinner plans. Most of the people who'd stayed late had already left for the night, while a few others declined ordering out. It was probably for the best, since she didn't need any greasy take-out. Chastity remembered a bowl of mixed fruit she'd left in the refrigerator and decided that would be a better option.

On her way to the kitchen, she stopped at Sebastian's door, wondering if she should check on him. Half of her said to keep moving, while the other half, wouldn't let her go on. Against her better judgment, Chastity knocked on the door.

"Come in." He wore a pair of gold-rimmed glasses, his nose buried in a pile of books. Sebastian looked just as sexy wearing them as he did without. Her pulse quickened, and as always, her body tightened with awareness. "What can I help you with, Chastity?"

"I was just peeking in to see if there was anything you needed, and to see if you were okay. That Pearl incident was intense."

He grimaced, pulling off his glasses and setting them aside. "I'm fine, thanks. Actually, I was more upset about the things she said about you."

Chastity shrugged. "She doesn't get to me most days."

"Her brand of harassment doesn't belong in the workplace, or anywhere else, for that matter. I would have said more to her, but it would only have exacerbated the situation. Don't worry about her, Chastity. It will be taken care of." He sighed, sounding as if he carried the weight of the world on his shoulders.

"Are you sure you're okay, Sebastian?"

A brief grin touched his lips, which didn't assure her at all. "I'm fine."

Not sure if she should press the issue, Chastity decided it was best to let it go. "Okay, but if you need something, let me know." When she made it to the door, a palm shot out, closing them inside together. Before she realized what was happening,

Sebastian turned her around and pushed her against the door. Then he covered her mouth in a hot, hungry kiss.

She wrapped her arms around his neck, pressing her body against the hard planes of his chest, surrendering to his forceful touch. His lips were firm and warm, the pressure increasing until she was breathless. Sebastian's tongue pushed against her slightly parted lips, taking full possession of her mouth.

Chastity clung to him helplessly, struggling to breathe. He'd never kissed her quite like this before. A slight feeling of desperation peeked through, yet her body still responded to his burning passion. His arms tightened around her in a heated vise. Chastity thought he might crush her, but pushing Sebastian away was the last thing she wanted to do.

Her soft moans of pleasure-pain were forced back by his savage tongue. His hands circled her throat before continuing on a path to her face. Finally they rested in her hair. Sebastian untied the ribbon holding her hair in place. Chastity felt the heavy weight of hair cascade around her shoulders.

He grabbed a hunk of it in his hand and pulled, yanking her head back, exposing her neck to his hungry gaze. Sebastian was a man possessed, the ungovernable lust within, barely contained. Her pussy clenched with need. They'd made love last night, but it still felt like forever since he'd last touched her.

Mind-jolting bursts of sensation flared throughout her. He trailed kisses along her throat, nibbling and sucking as though he wanted to leave his brand on her, declaring to the world that Chastity Bryant belonged to him. She placed her hands against his chest, reveling in his innate maleness.

Sebastian must have thought she was trying to break free because he finally lifted his head, pale green eyes flashing fire. "Don't push me away, dammit! I need this."

She caressed his chiseled jaw in a soothing motion. "I wasn't going to," Chastity whispered.

His eyes blazed with stark possession before he continued his tender assault. He pulled open her top with one furious yank. Chastity heard the popping of buttons flying and knew she'd have a hell of a time pulling herself together after this. Instinctively, she knew she couldn't stop him even if she wanted. Pushing her bra up, Sebastian freed her now highly sensitive breasts.

His hot mouth latched onto one puckered tip, sucking ferociously, the insistent pressure nearly causing pain, but she loved every single sizzling second of it. She dug her fingers into his hair, arching her back. "Oh, Sebastian, what are you doing to me?" Chastity groaned when he transferred his attention to her other nipple, licking and laving the hardened peak.

Sebastian raised her skirt, pushing it up to her waist. Before she realized what was happening, he dropped to his knees. "What are you doing?" she gasped.

"Doing something I've been thinking about doing all damn day."

She watched in fascination as his strong, muscled hands ripped her panties in two. "Sebastian!" she shrieked in surprise, but he ignored her protest. Pushing her legs apart and dividing the folds of her wet box, he circled her clit with his tongue.

Chastity placed her hands on his shoulders to steady herself as he tasted and worshipped the hot little button. "Oh God, Oh God, Oh God!" she moaned when his teeth grazed the sensitive nub and sucked it between his lips.

The intensity of her feelings flowed like honey, touching every nerve ending in her. She ground her pussy against his mouth in slow, sensual movements, as Sebastian continued his gentle torment, which brokered no resistance. His tongue glided along her slit in an almost loving motion, before he inserted two long fingers into her dripping channel. It didn't occur to Chastity to deny him, even when in the back of her mind she knew that there were still people in the office. Somehow that only heightened the pleasure.

She lifted a leg and slung it over Sebastian's shoulder when he buried his face deeper between her legs and slid cream-slicked fingers in and out of her juicy cunt. She rode his face with increasing urgency. When his mouth captured her clit again, Chastity exploded like a firecracker on the Fourth of July.

The mind-boggling sensation rocked her to the core, but Sebastian continued to eat her pussy like a starving man. "So delicious," he muttered, running his tongue from her clit to the crack of her ass.

"I don't think I can take anymore," she groaned. If his head remained between her legs any longer, she'd be reduced to nothing more than a quivering, boneless mass of nerves. He continued on, however, licking and sucking her to another earth-shattering climax. Only then did he stand to face her, a smug smile on his sculpted lips.

Chastity could barely see, her eyes clouded with desire. "Sebastian," she whispered weakly, not having the strength to move.

He stalked over to his desk and cleared it of everything except the computer. Then he returned to her. Grabbing Chastity by the hand, Sebastian led her to the desk before pushing her onto it.

She made a move to help him undo his pants, but he pushed her hands away. "I think if I let you touch me, I'm going to lose the last bit of control I have." His mouth twisted in a wry grin.

Chastity giggled. "I thought you'd already lost control."

"You haven't seen nothing yet, babe."

She waited impatiently for him to unleash that stiff cock straining against his pants. Unable to help herself, she trailed a finger along the outline of his erection. Sebastian stilled her hand. "Don't," he groaned.

She pouted, rubbing his crotch suggestively. "Let me."

Sebastian stepped back and undid his pants in fast, hurried motions. Since the incident in his kitchen, they didn't use condoms, and it only served to heighten the thrill of their joining. Pinioning Chastity on the desk, he gripped his shaft before guiding it into her.

She moaned as his thick, delicious cock sank deeper into her.

"So warm, so tight," he grunted. "I can stay inside of this pussy forever." His fingers dug into her thighs pulling them up, which caused him to go deeper still.

Chastity clenched her pussy muscles around his cock, making him moan. His balls slapped her ass as he pumped into her. She gripped Sebastian's arms, feeling the pulsing of his veins beneath her fingertips. "Oh, yes. Give it to me," she demanded, bucking her hips to meet him thrust for thrust.

Beads of sweat glistened on Sebastian's forehead, the abject look of passion on his face made Chastity shiver. With one more powerful push, a blazing orgasm tore through her body and she had to bite her lip to not scream. He began to shake, succumbing to his own forceful peak.

"Oh, God, Chastity! I love you!"

Her eyes sprang open. No. He couldn't have just said what she thought. His declaration would ruin everything. Chastity pushed him off, his semi-erect cock slipping out of her pussy. "No, Sebastian."

He frowned. "No what?"

"No, you didn't mean what you just said."

His expression grew stormy. "Like hell I didn't."

"But you can't love me. This wasn't...things weren't supposed to go this far."

Sebastian's eyes narrowed to green slits. "What are you talking about, Chastity?"

"You weren't supposed to love me...just...lust after me a bit."

"You're talking in circles. Don't tell me I don't love you, when my first thought in the morning and last one at night, is you. Hell, I think I've been halfway in love with you for months now."

"Months?" she asked dumbly. "That's not possible."

"Why isn't it?"

"Because you saw me as a frumpy mouse. You even laughed about it. Not once did you ever indicate having feelings for me."

"Because I didn't realize it until recently. I used to look forward to seeing your smiling face in the morning and missed it like hell when you stopped smiling at me. Hearing Pearl talk to you so disrespectfully made me realize that I don't want people to think this is some cheap affair."

"But, isn't that what this is?"

"No. It isn't."

Chastity slid off the desk and hurriedly adjusted her clothing the best she could, considering there were several missing buttons. She couldn't allow him into her heart, because if she did, there'd come a time when he'd grow tired of her too.

"Look, I need to get out of here. I've done most of the things on the list and I'll come in early to get the rest done."

Sebastian reached out, grabbing her wrist. "To hell with the list! This isn't over, Chastity."

She steeled herself against the conflicting feelings inside of her. It was breaking her heart. "Yes it is. This conversation is over and we're over. Now you know how it feels to be crushed. Doesn't feel so good, does it?"

His face lost all color, as he let go.

This was it. The moment of truth. If she didn't do it now, Chastity wouldn't have the strength to do it later on. Taking a deep breath, she tried to project a nonchalance she didn't feel. "What's the matter, Sebastian? Can't your ego take being dumped?"

Chapter Fifteen

"There's no way you're going to make that shot from half court." Jeremy shook his head, rubbing his sweat-drenched brow.

"I can and I will." Sebastian angled the ball toward the hoop.

"I smell a bet coming on."

"The only thing that smells are your ripe armpits."

"If I stink, so do you."

"It's quite possible, but watch me make this shot."

Jeremy laughed. "Fifty bucks says you won't."

"You're on." Sebastian released the ball and watched it fly across the court. The basketball hit the rim, bounced in the air, and hit the ground.

Jeremy threw his hands up in the air, waving them victoriously. "He throws up a brick!"

Sebastian shrugged, the shot hadn't been that important to him anyway. He really didn't want to be here right now. "Fine. I'll pay you as soon as I get my wallet."

The blond frowned. "You're not going to try to go best two out of three? Mr. Competitive himself?"

"You won. What more do you want?" Sebastian growled.

"What's wrong with you today, man? Every time I ask you something, I get short, curt answers and right now you have murder in your eyes. What gives?"

"Nothing!" Sebastian snapped.

"That's it! I'm taking my ball and going home. If you didn't want to come out tonight you should have said so, but your attitude I can do without. I don't deserve it." Jeremy stalked down the court to retrieve the basketball.

Sebastian raked his fingers through his hair. His friend was right. There was no call for his rudeness. "Jeremy, wait. I'm sorry. I know I'm being an ass, but...never mind. I'm sorry."

Jeremy stood in front of him, placing a hand on Sebastian's shoulder. "If there's something bothering you, then maybe you'll feel better getting it off your chest."

Should he open up about what a fool he'd been played for? Jeremy looked at him, concern etched on his face as he waited patiently for Sebastian to speak. Why the hell not? He'd have to deal with it eventually anyway. "It's Chastity."

"What about her? Aren't things going well with the two of you? I have to admit, I believed you'd lose interest after a few weeks like you usually do, but she's something special, isn't she?"

Sebastian snorted. "Yeah, so special that when I dropped the L-bomb, she threw it back in my face."

"Get the hell out of here! You told her you love her?"

"Yes, contrary to popular opinion, I do have feelings, you know."

"I'm not saying you don't, but what happened to your no-entanglements policy?"

"Chastity happened. I haven't been against the idea of love; I just never met anyone who made me feel like I do when I'm with her. Like I already told her, I think I've always been a little in love with her."

"Really? You used to call her a frump, and laughed at the fact she only talked about her cats."

"That's just it. I may have said those things, but some how, she was always on my mind. She's not the only paralegal in the firm who's reliable, but it was her I'd turn to. I think my subconscious knew what it took my heart too long to figure out."

"When you say she threw your love back in your face, what do you mean?"

"I mean, I told her that I loved her and she told me that we were through." Sebastian relayed every word that had been said up to the point when Chastity stormed out of his office, leaving him devastated.

"That doesn't sound like her. It just seems so callous. Is that exactly what she said?"

"Unfortunately."

Jeremy rubbed his chin as though deep in thought. "Something just doesn't make sense. You and I both suspected that she had a little bit of a thing for you, just by the way she used to act. Then all of a sudden, boom, here she comes looking like a black Jessica Rabbit. What happened to make her change, and I'm not just talking about appearance. I mean her personality."

"How the hell should I know? It's almost as if she set out to seduce me and then drop me. As a matter of fact..." Sebastian paused, as he remembered one crucial statement she'd made. *Because you saw me as a frumpy mouse. You laughed about it. How does it feel to be crushed?* Jeremy had just said something similar, but instinctively, Sebastian knew his friend hadn't betrayed his trust.

How did she know what he'd said about her unless...had she overheard a conversation he had? He racked his brain, trying to think of what he might had said to set her off like that.

"As a matter of fact, what?" Jeremy prompted.

"I think that's exactly what she did."

"I find that hard to believe, and if she did, what reason did she have to do it?"

"I'm thinking that she overheard me say something about her. I've never meant the things I said in a nasty way, or anything like that, but it's possible she could have taken it that way. Do you remember any conversations we had around the time she changed?"

"No—wait a minute. Do you remember that morning you were working on the Cochran case? You poked fun at Chastity and her cats. Now that I think about it, I thought I heard someone outside your door, and convinced myself that I'd imagined it."

Sebastian didn't feel any better knowing that everything he and Chastity had shared the past few months had been a lie. Granted, he was partly to blame for his callousness, but to be used like this hurt beyond anything imaginable. All the times they'd touched, kissed, fucked—no, made love—had meant absolutely nothing to her. Chastity had played him for a fool, and now Sebastian felt like a chump with a capital C.

Jeremy shot him a sympathetic look. "Are you going to be okay, man?"

"Would you be okay, if you fell in love with someone, only to find out that they were only with you for revenge? I thought I knew her, but I was wrong."

"What do you propose doing?"

Sebastian shrugged, his emotions threatening to choke him. "What can I do? I'll have to deal with it."

ಬಿಬಿಬಿ

"Chastity, sweetie, are you okay?" Dallas asked for the second time during the course of the meal.

"I'm fine!" she snapped. A silence fell across the table, and Chastity realized how bitchy that must have sounded. "I'm sorry, Dallas. That was uncalled for."

Dallas shook her head. "It's okay. I know you must have a lot on your mind, girl. Just consider me your sounding board."

Nick held up his champagne glass. "Shouldn't we be celebrating your victory? You showed that creep what's what." He laughed, dramatically flipping a lock of curly brown hair off his face, his gray eyes twinkling with mischief.

"If I'm the victor, why do I feel like such a loser? I should have backed out before things went too far. You guys didn't see the look on his face when I dropped the proverbial bomb on him." Chastity pushed her plate away, her appetite gone.

Dallas reached for her hand. "But, isn't this what you wanted?"

Chastity sighed. "To be honest, no. This is what you guys wanted." She laughed without humor. "But ultimately it's my fault, because I very well could have said no, but something within me wanted to show Sebastian that I could be a desirable woman too. What I didn't count on was falling even harder for him than I had before." She didn't miss the silent exchange between her three friends, and pretty much knew what they were thinking.

"Look guys, I made assumptions about him before I went into this whole thing. I thought that whatever he had coming to him he deserved, but as I spent more time with Sebastian, I saw his kinder, gentler side. Whenever we'd make love, he'd hold me and tell me how beautiful I am. He'd send me thoughtful little gifts. One time, I told him about a book I wanted to read. The next day, he had it waiting on my desk when I arrived at work. On top of that, when I was sick, he took care of me and even watched my cats, even though I know he hates them. I fell for him all over again, but all my old feelings of inadequacy reared its head and I got scared."

"Scared of what?" Kevin asked gently.

"Scared that he'd eventually get tired of me! Even with this new look, I never completely believed in myself, especially when it came to him." Chastity wanted to cry, but didn't want to embarrass herself in front of her friends. "Excuse me. I need to run to the ladies room."

Dallas made a move to get up with her, but Chastity held her hand up. "That's okay. I'd rather just go by myself."

"Are you sure?" her friend persisted.

"Yes. Just give me a few minutes." Once in the restroom, Chastity splashed some water on her face and then patted it dry. The reflection staring back at her was one she was still getting used to. Aesthetically, she was more pleasing to the eye, but she'd always be the same old Chastity. She liked that girl so much better than what she'd become. So what if her life hadn't been exciting and full of dates, it was hers, and she'd been content.

No matter what, she owed Sebastian an apology. Regardless of what he may have said, no one deserved to be hurt the way she'd done him. Not to mention that she ended up hurting herself in the process. Maybe he'd accept her apology, or maybe not, but at least she'd be able to move on.

Damn.

She wished it didn't hurt so much. Chastity repaired her make-up and headed out of the bathroom. Shock halted her, to see Sebastian coming out of the men's restroom. The look on his face told her that he was just as surprised to see her here, as she was him.

"Sebastian!"

Light green eyes hardened to narrowed flints briefly, before his mouth relaxed into a mocking grin. "Well, well, well. Chastity, you're looking well. Are you here tonight to celebrate your victory?"

She faltered at the mention of what she did to him. Fists clenching and unclenching by her side, Chastity fought to remain composed. "That's hardly fair, Sebastian."

"Oh, I don't know about that, but if you've suddenly developed a guilty conscience, then don't. Actually, I have a lot to thank you for."

She frowned. "What for?"

"You showed me that what I believed I felt for you couldn't possibly be real. I gave it a lot of thought and realized, I don't want to be tied down to just one woman. Come with me, and I'll show you what I mean." Sebastian took hold of her elbow, leading Chastity out to the dining area. She struggled to break free of his vise grip, to no avail. They stopped where a bored-looking redhead sat.

The woman had to be one of the most stunning females Chastity had ever seen, making her feel gauche and awkward just standing there. The woman's dark blue gaze slid up and down Chastity's body within a couple seconds, and by the quick dismissal, found her lacking. Completely ignoring Chastity, the redhead looked at Sebastian and pouted. "Sebastian, what took you so long?"

"Oh, I ran into one of my employees. Marcy this is Chastity." He introduced the two women as if butter wouldn't melt in his mouth.

His employee? Chastity's face flamed with embarrassment. Marcy gave her a brief nod of acknowledgement. Barely.

"Nice to meet you," Chastity mumbled. "I have to get back to my table."

As she turned away, Sebastian grasped her wrist, halting her, and then leaned over until his lips practically touched her ear. "I thought it was only fitting that you meet your replacement. I have to thank you for showing me the error of my foolishness. And I'm sure later on tonight, Marcy will thank you, too."

Chastity didn't know how she maintained her composure, but she managed to keep her face impassive as Sebastian searched it for a reaction. "Enjoy the rest of your dinner, Sebastian," she replied quietly, clinging as tightly as she could to her dignity. With a swift tug, she freed herself from his grasp and walked away.

Fighting the urge to spare him one last glance, she made it back to her table on wobbly legs. Her friends, who'd been laughing and carrying on, stopped when she took a seat.

"What's wrong, Chas?" Dallas asked with a frown.

"I think I need to go home. I'm not feeling well right now."

"Of course. Let's get the bill and we'll take you home," Kevin agreed. "Is it your stomach, head or both? I thought the calamari might have tasted a little off."

"Headache," she lied. She very well couldn't say heartache. "Please, can I just get out of here now? I think a little air will do me good."

"Okay. Let me go to the restroom first and I'll come with you," Dallas offered.

Kevin threw a few fifties on the table, and kissed Nick on the neck. "I'll walk Chas outside. You don't mind waiting for the check to come, do you?"

"No, go ahead." Nick winked at Chastity. "Feel better, babe."

"Thanks, Nick." She gave him a weak smile as she stood.

Kevin casually slung his arm around her shoulder as they walked out the restaurant. Just as they stepped outside, Chastity froze when she spied Sebastian and his date in a passionate embrace. It was at that moment, when he lifted his head, with lipstick smudged lips. The amusement in his eyes soon turned hard and cold, as he saw who stood next to her.

Chastity gripped Kevin's arm protectively, looking away. Let Sebastian think what he wanted. At least then she could walk away with her pride. Seeing him holding another woman the way he had, stung her to the core. It felt as if her heart had been ripped into tatters of confetti. Biting her inner lip to hold in a sob, Chastity clutched the front of her shirt, trying to still the pounding of her heart.

"Chas, are you okay?"

"I'm okay. The sooner I get home, the better I'll be."

"It doesn't have anything to do with the Italian Stallion over there, does it?"

She gasped, meeting knowing brown eyes. "You know?"

"I saw him enter the restaurant with his little friend. If you ask me, darling, she has nothing on you."

"Why didn't you say anything when you saw him?"

"I didn't recognize him at first, but I did when I just saw him now. Chas, hon, you have it bad, don't you?"

"Is it obvious?"

He smiled gently. "Just a little."

"What do you think I should do? I tried to apologize to him, but he didn't want to hear it. I think it may be best if I just start looking for another job."

"You're going to run away? That's the coward's way out."

"Maybe it is, but I don't think I can take seeing him parade all those women into the office again. It would hurt too much." Before she could stop it, a tear slid down her face. Kevin pulled her into his arms, rocking Chastity back and forth. "You know, Kevin, when this entire thing started, I was just trying to get my own back. Then when I realized how much I was falling for him, not just the silly schoolgirl crush I had before, I started worrying about getting hurt. I tried to protect my heart, but I ended up getting hurt anyway. Now I have to figure out how to stop loving him."

Chapter Sixteen

"Thank you, Mrs. Carter. I'll be getting in contact with you within the next couple days or so, to let you know if we have a case. From what you're telling me, it does sound like the doctor was negligible, to some extent. You have to remember though, that if you're found even partially liable for what happened, the reward you want may not be as large as you'd like it to be. From what I can see, the hospital is offering a very fair sum, considering it was your responsibility to follow up with them. They could argue that, had you come back for your check up, you wouldn't have suffered that mild heart attack. Besides that, you didn't take the medication the doctor prescribed, and by your own admission, you're a smoker."

"Are you trying to tell me I don't have a case? If I don't, then why are they offering me blood money? My cousin Marty's son, David, is in his second year of law school and David thinks I have a case. Are you trying to say a law student knows more than you do?"

Sebastian bit the inside of his lip to keep an angry retort back. There was nothing more annoying than someone who thought they knew his job better than he did. He could already see that it would be a nightmare working with this woman. Fortunately, he had enough business to decline her if he chose. In fact, the only reason he'd agreed to see Mrs. Carter, was because he owed an old friend a favor. "I'm not saying one way or the other. In order for me to ascertain that information, I'll have to subpoena the hospital records."

"At one hundred and fifty dollars an hour? I'll end up owing more than I'll probably get. That's robbery."

"You'd only owe the consultation fee. I wouldn't start the hourly rate until we had a contract."

"Hmph. My son says you're one of the best, but I see no evidence of that so far." The woman crossed her arms, a ferocious frown on her saggy face.

"I'm sorry you feel that way. Perhaps I might not be the best person to represent your case."

Mrs. Carter's mouth dropped open, giving her the look of a hooked fish. Sebastian knew the game she was playing. She didn't want to pay the consultation fee and he'd just called her bluff.

"So, just like that, you're willing to throw away my business?"

"I'm not saying that at all, but I think you're looking for a quick yes or no, and I'm not willing to give you that without any further investigation."

The woman gathered her belongings in a huff and stood up. "Thanks for nothing. I'm sure there are plenty of attorneys who would help me out."

"I'm sure there are," Sebastian agreed, trying to keep the boredom out of his voice. He wished she'd hurry up and leave.

Mrs. Carter's eyes narrowed. "So, that's it then? You would rather I walk out the door, than retain me as a client?"

Exactly.

"Ma'am, if it's your intention to leave, I don't see how I can convince you otherwise. I wish you luck with your suit."

Her face flushed, then turned beet red. Obviously she'd expected him to beg. "Well, I'll certainly let my son know that you're not as competent as he claims you are."

Sebastian breathed a sigh of relief when she slammed the door behind her. He needed no further complications as it was. His professional life may have been a ten, but his personal life was a one, and it didn't help matters to see Chastity in the office day in and out. Maybe it would be best if she wasn't here, but the very thought caused him pain. He didn't know if he was coming or going.

He was finding it more difficult, with each passing day, to ignore his feelings, no matter how hard he tried. He'd dated other women to get her out of his system, but all he could do was think of her. Sebastian's date with Marcy had ended disastrously when he'd called her by Chastity's name. He hasn't been laid in weeks, and it was all Chastity's fault!

Sebastian picked up the pile of mail he'd ignored all morning and began shuffling through it, pausing when he came across an envelope with only his name on it. What was this? Taking out the carefully folded piece of paper inside, his eyes scanned its contents. When he finished it, he felt like someone had slammed a fist into his stomach.

No. This couldn't be what he thought it was. Pushing away from his desk, he stormed out of his office and stalked toward Chastity's desk. Slapping the paper on her desk, he demanded, "What the hell is this?"

Not bothering to raise her head as she continued typing whatever she was working on, Chastity said, "I would have thought that was obvious. It's my notice."

"You know what I mean, dammit, and would you at least have the decency to look at me when you're speaking?"

She looked in his direction then, revealing tear-swollen eyes. Her face was bare of make-up, other than a clear lip gloss. Even when she wasn't dolled up, she was beautiful. Why hadn't he noticed a long time ago, and why had she been crying? Most of his anger abated at the sadness on her face. "Chastity?"

"Please don't make this harder than this has to be. I...I think it's for the best."

"But..." He wanted to ask her to stay, plead and tell her he loved her, but wounded pride wouldn't allow it. Instead he said, "With Pearl gone, we'll be down two paralegals if you leave. It's a rather inopportune time for you to put in your notice. Besides, I never pegged you for a coward."

She sighed, sounding weary. "What are you talking about, Sebastian?"

"You're the one who started this little game of revenge." A humorless smile tugged at the corner of his lips when he gauged her startled reaction. "Oh, yeah. You didn't think I'd figure it out, did you? Well, I did. I know I hurt your feelings, and for that I'm truly sorry, but you set out to destroy me, didn't you?"

"I..."

"Didn't you!" he yelled, drawing curious stares in their direction.

"This isn't the place to have this discussion."

"Fine." Grabbing her by the arm, he pulled her down the hall and led her outside. "Now, answer my question."

She shook her head vehemently. "I never expected it to go to the extreme that it did. I didn't think you...I'm sorry," she whispered, her misery apparent.

Good. He wanted her to suffer as much as he did. "You and your boyfriend must have had a good laugh at my expense."

"Kevin isn't my boyfriend, I swear."

"Spare me your lies. I've had enough of them. I thought you were special. You were the first woman who I dreamed of having a future with. No matter what your motivation, I know you felt something for me. Maybe it wasn't love, but you'll remember the nights when we made love until we were blind and deaf to the world. I hope that gives you something to think about." He paused, taking in her ashen expression, knowing he could stop right there, but the need to lash out drove him.

"You know, I could almost respect you for your stand, but this last act of cowardice makes me realize you're not the person I thought you were. You're not even a woman. You're a little girl playing dress up." Sebastian refused to be moved by the sheer pain within the depths of her dark eyes, a pain that mirrored his own. "If it's your wish to leave this firm, you can do so, starting today. You'll be paid in lieu of notice. Good luck...Miss Bryant."

౷౷౷

Chastity's head ached and she wanted to cry. She wondered how she'd even managed to go grocery shopping feeling the way she did, as she tossed the bag on the table before plopping down on the sofa. She was exhausted. After a long day at work, all she wanted to do was sleep. It was only day three at her new job, and she was already considering looking for something else.

It paid a few thousand dollars less and the firm was much larger. Some of the partners were nice, while others thought their shit didn't stink. One particular attorney at the firm thought it was beneath him to make eye contact with her as he spoke, but had no problem staring at her chest.

Chastity felt like showering whenever he was around. Still, it was slightly better than seeing Sebastian day in and out, and wanting him. She'd had a lot of time to reflect on his last words to her. He was right.

She was a coward.

She'd fallen just as hard for him, but refused to admit it. At least Sebastian had the guts to lay his heart on the line. She, on the other hand, had run away.

Monty stalked over to her, rubbing his body against her leg. She still had her cats, at least. How pathetic. Chastity was just about to get up and put the groceries away, when the doorbell rang.

Frowning, she wondered who it could be. Nick and Kevin were in New York on vacation, and Dallas had gone down South to deal with a family crisis. Chastity didn't want to answer the door, but whoever it was, didn't seem to want to go away. Peeking through the peephole, she was surprised to see who her visitor was.

"Jeremy? What are you doing here?" she asked, as she opened the door.

He wore a grim expression. "May I come in?" he asked formally, ignoring her question.

"Uh, yeah, sure."

"Would you like something to drink?" Chastity offered, once he was inside.

"No, thanks. This isn't really a social call."

"At least have a seat. You're making me nervous, pacing around like that. Besides, you're about to—"

Rarrh! Grrrrr...

"...step on my cat's tail," she finished weakly.

Monty wasn't the type to run from a fight. With a swipe of his paw, he sliced through the khaki material of Jeremy's pants. "What the—get this hellcat away from me," he protested, as Monty swiped him again, and then to add insult to injury, bit the stunned man.

"Monty, no!" Chastity lifted the hissing cat and took him to the bedroom, shutting him in. "I'm really sorry about that. He thinks he's much bigger than he actually is."

"How you deal with such a beast is beyond me."

"Well, you did step on his tail," she pointed out.

Raking fingers through his blond hair, he sighed. "So, I did. I apologize."

"Did he draw blood? Are you hurt?"

"I'm fine. It's a good thing I'm not wearing shorts. That cat is vicious." He took a seat on the sofa. "I'm sure you know why I've come."

"No. Actually, I don't, since I asked you what you were doing here when I opened the door, but you chose to ignore my question." Chastity sat next to him.

"Sebastian is the reason I'm here."

"Does he know you're here?"

"Hell no! If he did, he'd probably beat me to a bloody pulp."

"I see."

"Do you really?" He raised one dark blond brow.

"Honestly? No, but I'm sure you'll enlighten me on the reason you've decided to come on Sebastian's behalf, without his knowledge."

"Chastity, I didn't come here to spar words with you. Sebastian's in a bad way."

Chastity's heart skipped a beat. "What do you mean, a bad way? Has he been hurt?"

Jeremy shook his head. "No. Nothing like that, but he's not the same guy he was before you set out to play the avenger."

"That's not what I set out to do."

"Oh, really? From where I'm sitting, it looks to me like that's exactly what you did."

"If you've come to hurl accusations at me, then I'd rather you left. I don't need this." She stood up, but to her surprise Jeremy grabbed her wrist, yanking Chastity back down on the sofa.

"I'm not going to let you walk away, until this situation is resolved."

"Let go of me," she hissed.

Immediately he released her, but the angry glare still remained. "Was what he said worth you doing what you did to him?"

"I don't know what you're talking about," she lied.

"Do me a favor; don't insult my intelligence. We've already figured that you must have overheard us talking. So, I ask again, was what he said worth doing what you did?"

Chastity poked her bottom lip out mutinously before her shoulders slumped and head drooped. "I didn't think he'd fall in love with me."

"What did you think would happen when you paraded yourself in front of him the way you did?"

"I just thought he'd be interested for as long as someone like him, can be. I only planned to flirt with him a little, maybe go on a few dates together before I dumped him, but that's as far as I planned on going."

"So, why did you let things progress?"

"Why do you want to know? What's the point of dredging this up?"

"Because he's my best friend and I don't like seeing him hurt."

"Like he's hurt so many women before, with his love them and leave them ways?" she snapped.

"How the hell would you know that? Those women meant nothing to him, and every single one of them knew the deal. Sebastian doesn't have to play games, like you obviously do."

That comment hit its mark, but she'd made her bed. "What's done is done. What do you expect me to do? I tried to apologize, but he brushed it off. In fact, he seemed happy that I didn't return his love. He told me that he wasn't ready to settle down."

Jeremy rolled his eyes heavenward. "Can't you recognize an act when you see one? The man is miserable. He spends all his time holed up in his office, he's short with people, he's lost weight, and he's apathetic about everything. You served him a raw deal, Chastity."

She briefly remembered the flash of pain she'd seen in his eyes when she'd rejected him. "I'm sorry I hurt him. Like I said, I tried to apologize. He seemed fine. I don't work for your firm anymore, so you might as well just write me off. This was a wasted trip for you."

He stood up, the disgust evident on his face. "I was hoping that by coming here, you might...it doesn't matter what I thought anymore, but I'll tell you what I know. There was a time, when you may not have been the most glamorous of women, but that didn't matter because you were a sweet lady. Your appearance isn't the only thing that changed. You may look hot, but your insides don't make you very appealing right now. Hopefully it won't take Sebastian much longer to get over what you did, because he's much better off without a schemer like you in his life."

Jeremy's words hit her deep. She shouldn't have hurt Sebastian the way she did. Burying her face in her hands, Chastity let out a sob. Jeremy released a loud curse before sitting back down and throwing an arm around her. "Don't cry, Chastity. I didn't mean to upset you."

"Liar," she croaked.

"Okay," he conceded. "Maybe just a little bit."

"I didn't really change that much. I just made a lot of stupid decisions. When I overheard Sebastian laughing about my lack of a life, I was crushed. It cut deep, so my friends and I came up with a plan to make me over, and then set out to seduce Sebastian. It was all just fun and games to me, at first. I just didn't realize it would work so well, and I definitely hadn't counted on his feelings. What started out as revenge became real. I...fell in love with him, too."

"Then why did you hurt him the way you did?"

"Because I didn't believe in myself enough to trust the love he'd offered me. I was a big, fat coward. Now, it's too late, because he's moved on."

"Haven't you been listening to what I said, woman? He hasn't moved on. He's still nuts over you."

Chastity shook her head in disbelief. "Well, he has a funny way of showing it."

"Did you expect him to wear his heart on his sleeve after you crushed him?"

She sighed. "I guess not. But, what can I do about it now?"

"You say you love him."

"I do."

"Then prove it. Fight for him. It may not be easy, because Sebastian can be a stubborn sonofabitch when he wants to be, but I know he still loves you. I've never seen him as happy as the times he was with you." Jeremy patted her hand in reassurance.

Chastity knew then what she had to do.

Chapter Seventeen

Sebastian downed his third glass of vodka, letting the warm liquid burn a trail down his throat. Damn. He wished he didn't have such a high tolerance for alcohol. What he needed was to get stinking drunk. Maybe then, he could push the pain he felt to the furthest recesses of his mind.

He hadn't seen Chastity in a month, but he hurt just as much now as he did on the day when she'd taken his heart and crushed it beneath her designer heels. Still, he couldn't help thinking about her gorgeous breasts, crowned with nipples so dark and tempting they made his mouth water.

His cock twitched as he remembered how she'd sighed and moaned his name when he slid into her tight, fragrant pussy. Sebastian had made several attempts to date other women, but none of them could make him forget Chastity. Hell, he could barely bring himself to even look at another woman.

She'd emasculated him and didn't have the decency to stick around and brazen the whole damn thing out. If she were here right now, he'd...he'd...ring her pretty little neck and then beg her to love him. It was kind of sad, but there it was. God, she'd reduced him to an emotional mess.

He couldn't go on like this. He'd have to learn to live without her...if he could. He reached for the bottle of vodka to pour himself another drink, when the doorbell rang. Who the hell was that? "Go away," he muttered, only the visitor didn't go away. The persistent ringing of the bell told him that he'd either have to answer it or call the police.

Not bothering to look through the peephole, he wrenched the door open, and stumbled back in surprise when he saw who stood on the other side. "Chastity." He must have been drunker than he thought, because surely he was imagining things.

Even casually dressed, she looked beautiful to him. His fingers itched to caress every inch of her silky smooth skin. She wore a pair of jeans that hugged curvaceous hips, and a tight T-shirt, which didn't help matters either. Sebastian licked his lips as he spied the outline of her bra through it, knowing the treasure they supported within.

His body tensed with awareness. No. He wouldn't let this she-devil under his skin this way, but looking down into her big brown eyes, he wanted to pull her into his arms. *Keep your cool, Sebastian.* "What the hell do you want?"

"May I come in?"

"For what? I see no reason to let you in."

With downcast eyes, Chastity sighed. "Because, I'd like to talk to you."

"So talk. I'm not stopping you."

"I was hoping you'd let me in first."

It was clear she wouldn't leave without her pound of flesh. He may as well get this over with. "Fine, come in, but whatever you have to say, how about wrapping it up in five minutes," he growled, standing back just enough to let her in. He nearly grabbed Chastity as the scent of her perfume wafted to his nostrils.

He walked back to the living room and took a seat on the couch, not bothering to offer her a seat. Chastity looked around, probably taking in the mess he'd made, and frowned. "Sebastian, how much have you had to drink?"

"Not that it's any of your goddamn business, but I'm working on my fourth glass."

"Maybe you should stop."

Was she for real? It almost sounded as if she cared.

"If I need someone to lecture me, I'll call my mother. From my estimation, you've just wasted two of your five minutes, so either tell me what you want, or leave," he barked. Just having her there made him want things to be the way they were before she'd played that trick on him.

Stay strong, he warned himself again.

"I came here to ask for your forgiveness. What I did was wrong and I'm very sorry that I caused you pain." Chastity began quietly, shifting back and forth on her feet.

Yes, Sebastian wanted to scream, but he forced himself to remember how cruelly she'd rejected him. "Okay, apology accepted. Now that you've had your say, you can go." Inwardly, he congratulated himself for remaining cool, when he was so close to crumbling.

"Please, that's not all. I wanted to tell you...oh, hell," she broke off in apparent frustration. "I love you, Sebastian! I'm deeply, madly, and irrevocably in love with you. I have been for a while now, but I just didn't know how to tell you. It's true that I made myself over to get your attention, but I never meant to let things go as far as they had. The more time I spent with you, however, the harder I fell. I got to know the man you truly are, and not just the one I'd only idolized before."

Sebastian's heart sped up. Was what she said true? Part of him wanted to jump off the couch and press kisses all over her tempting body, but caution kept him glued to the spot. "Is that so? You have a funny way of showing someone you love them.

For the sake of hoots and giggles, let's say I believe you. What did you wish to accomplish by telling me this? Did you think I'd actually return that love?"

Chastity nibbled on her bottom lip, her nervous gesture making his cock stir. Sebastian shifted his weight to ease the uncomfortable ache.

"I...I was hoping that you would, still love me, I mean. You were right to call me a coward, because I was. I was just so scared that you'd eventually lose interest in me, that I didn't give our love a chance. I didn't realize then, that love is all about taking risks, and laying your heart on the line. You understood that. I was a fool." She walked up to him and knelt, her dark eyes looking up at him imploringly. "I love you, Sebastian. It breaks my heart when I think about how much I hurt you. Believe it or not, it hurt me, too. Tell me that I have a chance."

Sebastian clenched and unclenched his fists. He wanted to believe her, but the taunting words of her rejection seared through his mind. *What's the matter, Sebastian? Can't your ego take being dumped?*

He lifted a brow. "I don't really know what to tell you, Chastity. I kind of like playing the field. There are just too many women out there...willing and waiting. I really don't see why I should oblige, especially for you."

Chastity clutched his hand. "I'll take whatever I can get from you. If no strings attached sex is all you want from me, then fine. I'm willing to do that, but please don't send me away." Tears glistened in her eyes, threatening to spill.

His resistance was faltering, but he still needed to be sure of her.

"So, if I called in the middle of the night, and asked you to come over for a midnight fuck, would you?"

She nodded, wiping away a tear that had escaped.

"And then if I told you to leave afterwards? What would you do?"

"If that's what you wanted, I'd leave."

"Would you let me fuck you anytime, anywhere...any hole I wanted?"

"Yes," Chastity answered, barely above a whisper.

"And you wouldn't expect anything else from me?"

"No."

"And what if I want to date other women?"

"I'd be lying if I said I wouldn't mind the other women, but if I have to share you, then so be it. I'll...I won't like it, but I won't make a fuss about it."

He had her just where he wanted her. "That sounds nice, but you're going to have to back those words up with some action."

She gulped. "What do you want me to do?"

"Stand up and get undressed. I want to see if you're even worth the effort."

Chastity flinched. Those words sounded harsh, even to his ears, but it was like a devil riding him. Slowly, she rose to her feet and took a few steps back. Sebastian's breathing grew shallow as she lifted the T-shirt over her head. This was what he'd been waiting for.

Chastity forced herself to stop trembling. Sebastian was out for blood, but she knew this was what she deserved. The time had come for her to grow up and stop being afraid. She loved this man with every fiber in her being. If this was what it took to be a part of his life, then she'd do it.

"Slower," he commanded, as she tossed the T-shirt aside. She trembled as his green gaze slid up and down her body insolently. Shame burned through her, as her nipples tightened. Chastity wanted his hands on her so badly she thought she'd faint with need, but she dared not move unless he spoke.

"Very nice. Now take off your jeans, and this time, don't go so fast."

She knew he was intentionally trying to humiliate her, but it didn't stop the excitement racing through her. Discarding the jeans, Chastity licked suddenly dry lips. Sebastian wasn't giving anything away. She couldn't gauge his reaction. Had Jeremy been wrong? Maybe Sebastian had gotten over her.

No. Don't talk yourself out of this, Chastity. Fight for him.

"Chickening out, Chastity?" Sebastian taunted.

"No."

He chuckled. "It seems you have more guts than I thought. Now, take off the bra and panties."

She hesitated briefly, wondering if he'd come to her now. She finally stood naked, waiting for what he'd do next. Why didn't he move? "Sebastian?" she asked tentatively.

"I've decided I won't take you up on your offer, after all. I don't want you in that capacity."

Chastity's heart plummeted. Is this how Sebastian had felt when he'd laid his heart on the line? Tears scalded her cheeks, but she refused to leave until he said the words.

"Okay," she whispered. "In what capacity do you want me?"

He stood then and stalked toward her like a jungle cat locked on his prey. "So compliant. I like that." Sebastian trailed a finger across her breast. Chastity gasped as bolts of desire flickered through her body. "Will you give me anything I ask for?" he asked, lightly pinching one hardened tip. Her pussy clenched with need, as she mashed her thighs together to temper the aching heat.

"Anything," she promised.

He cupped her sensitive mounds in his palms, his thumbs grazing each tip. It felt like forever since she'd been touched like this. Chastity desperately wanted to throw her arms around him, but Sebastian called all the shots right now. Closing her eyes, Chastity savored the delicious sensations zipping along every single nerve ending.

"What if I want your love?" he asked softly.

Chastity's eyes shot open. If he was playing games, she wished he'd hurry up and end this torture. "You have it. With all my heart."

"Good. Because I'll settle for nothing less than a committed relationship from you." His words stunned her so much, that she didn't immediately react when Sebastian pulled her into his arms, and started raining kisses all over her face and neck. "I love you so much, Chastity. You have no idea how much I've missed you."

Before she could respond, his mouth covered hers in a hungry kiss, his tongue shooting past her lips. She clung to him, pressing her body against his, reveling at the feeling of being in his arms again.

Chastity returned the kiss, her tongue darting out to meet his in a syncopated dance of lust. Sebastian's erection pressed against her stomach. Lord, she missed this. Right now, there was nothing she wanted more than to feel his cock sliding into her slick channel, but there were still things that needed to be resolved.

Reluctantly she tore her mouth away from his with a laugh. "Sebastian, let me catch my breath."

"No." He cupped her face, capturing her bottom lip with strong white teeth. Chastity placed her palms against his chest, meaning to push him away, but then his hands slid down her body to cup her ass. She was lost. Sebastian ground his cock against the juncture of her thighs, and she wished he was naked too.

He lifted his head after what seemed like an eternity. "Chastity, I missed you, so much."

She caressed the side of his face. "I missed you, too. I love you."

"Say that again."

"I love you."

"If you ever leave me again, I swear to God, I'll hunt you down and lock you in the basement, only letting you out to make love."

Pain lanced through her heart when she thought of what she did. "I'm so sorry to have caused you so much pain. It was a stupid reason to do what I did."

"Only if you can forgive me for being such a pompous ass. I have to admit, that I shouldn't have taken advantage of your kindness in the first place. I had a lot of time to think about what I did to you, and I'm not proud of myself. As my mother and Jeremy have told me on countless occasions I can be a son of a bitch. Thank you for loving me, sweetheart."

"But what I did was inexcusable, I reinvented myself into someone I didn't like very much."

"Bite your tongue, woman, I liked that woman very much." He laughed, giving her a light kiss on the forehead.

Chastity frowned. "You did?"

"Oh, I'm not talking about the glammed-out diva, although the appearance was pretty sexy. I'm referring to the sweet

Chastity, whose eyes lit up with wonder whenever we made love, and the one who'd lay her head so sweetly in my lap after I had a long, hard day."

Her heart swelled with love. This time when she cried, they were tears of joy. "I can't believe this is happening. I thought I'd lost you."

Sebastian engulfed her in his arms, burying his face against her neck. "You couldn't lose me if you tried. I want to spend the rest of my life with you."

"Are you...are you..."

"Asking you to marry me?"

"Yes. Are you?" She'd never pictured being proposed to like this, while she was buck naked, but there was nothing she could think of that would make her happier than being Sebastian's wife.

"No. I'm telling you we're getting married. When I get the chance, I'll do it right with the flowers and the ring and hoopla, but I want you to know my intentions right here and now. I want it all. You, a couple kids, or however many you want. I'll even take your damn cats to have you in my life."

Chastity didn't think she could love him any more than she did right now. Chastity Rossi. That had a nice ring to it. "Sebastian, I don't need pomp and circumstance. I only need you. What will your mom say?"

"She'll love you, because I do."

"What about the other women?" she asked, still not believing this was all real.

He shook his head. "There've never been any other women, since you. I only went on one date with Marcy, and that was it."

She smacked him playfully on the shoulder. "You had me believing that you'd moved on."

A sheepish grin split Sebastian's handsome face. God she loved this man. "I'm sorry about that little lie, my love, but my pride wouldn't allow me to admit how badly I hurt. Were you jealous?"

"Terribly. Tell me where you hurt, Sebastian and I'll make it better."

He pointed to a place with his finger over his heart. Chastity pressed her lips against that point. "Better?" she asked.

"It's definitely getting there. And what about you and your friend, Kevin?"

"Jealous?" she teased him with his own taunt.

"I wanted to rip his damn heart out."

Chastity laughed. "Kevin is definitely the last person you'd ever have to be worried about. Besides being one of my best friends, he's in a committed relationship with his boyfriend Nick."

Sebastian's jaw dropped momentarily. "That guy is gay?"

"If he isn't, his boyfriend certainly is," she laughed.

"Why you...do you have any idea what you put me through? I would lay awake at night imagining you with him and it would eat me up inside."

She stood on her tiptoes and pressed her lips against his. "Now you can put your nights to better use."

"Oh, I intend to." He scooped her up in his arms. "Starting now. I hope you don't have plans on getting a lot of sleep tonight, because we have a lot to make up for."

Chastity wrapped her arms around Sebastian's neck as he carried her to his bedroom. Despite her glamorous makeover, Chastity learned that the real catalyst that led to her complete transformation was love. The caterpillar was now a full-fledge butterfly.

About the Author

To learn more about Eve Vaughn, please visit www.evevaughn.com Send an email to Eve at eve@evevaughn.com or join her Yahoo! group to join in the fun with other readers as well as Eve. http://groups.yahoo.com/group/evevaughnsbooks

Look for these titles

Now Available

The Life and Loves of April Johnson
A Night to Remember

An old-fashioned undertaker who asks for lessons in what turns a woman on...what more could any teacher ask for?

Mortified Matchmaker
© 2007 Alexis Fleming

When circumstances force kindergarten teacher Melissa Morgan to take her twin sister's place as proprietor of a dating agency, the last thing she expects is to meet a funeral director in desperate need of lessons in what a woman wants. Despite his quirky behavior and antiquated ideas, Matthew Campbell pushes every one of Melissa's buttons and it's not long before the lessons become more important than finding Matthew a mate.

But how will Melissa react when she finds out Matthew is an undercover federal agent in pursuit of a blackmailer and she's the prime suspect?

Available now in ebook and print from Samhain Publishing.

Enjoy the following excerpt from Mortified Matchmaker...

"Make yourself comfortable, Matthew, and I'll put the first of the tapes on."

Wobbling slightly as the unfamiliar high heels caught in the thick pile of the carpet, she moved to the far end of the room, slid the video into the machine and turned on the television. Remote control in hand, she joined Matthew on the sofa and started the tape.

"This first lady's name is Martha Frazer. She's perhaps a little older than you specified on your application form, but she sounds very much a homebody. Anyway, I'll let you view the tape and you can tell me what you think."

As Matthew watched the screen, Melissa tried to find a comfortable position on the sofa. With it being so wide, she couldn't lean back against the cushions. If she did, she'd have to sit with her legs extended out in front of her like a child. Not very professional.

Neither was the flash of garters high on her thighs as she tried to perch on the extreme edge of the sofa. She tugged at the hemline of her skirt, only to have it ride up again as soon as she released it. Hell, at this rate, she'd be forced to sit with both hands on the bottom of her skirt to keep it in place.

As the video ended, she turned to Matthew, an enquiring look on her face. "So what do you think?"

Matt tried not to grin as her skirt slid up to expose the top of her nylons and gave him a quick glimpse of naked thigh. He'd seen her efforts to tweak it down. If she didn't want her legs on show, why wear such short skirts?

The character Joshua Cribbs had created for him foremost in his mind, Matt clasped his hands together and lowered his chin to tap at his pursed lips with pointed index fingers. "Hmm, she sounds a very nice lady," he said.

"But?"

"I'm not certain she's suitable. Very unfashionable and a lot older than I wanted. Probably set in her ways. Not malleable at all. I don't think I'd be able to mold her into what I perceive as the perfect partner."

He knew his words sounded chauvinistic, but it suited his undercover identity. With his Italian heritage, he was used to a culture where women were revered, feted and looked after. Although that in itself sounded chauvinistic, the women in his family were strong and independent, equal partners in any relationship.

Still, he had a part to play and somehow he had to get Mel Morgan to take him personally under her wing, not fob him off on one of her clients. If he took these women on a date and screwed it up, maybe they'd report back to Melissa. Then he could suggest she teach him how to romance a woman. He couldn't think of any other way to get close enough to Miss Morgan to find out what he needed to know.

"You know, perhaps I've been going about this the wrong way. I think I need someone more glamorous. I'd like to lift the profile of my business, and as I'd want any prospective partner to work with me, at least until the children come, perhaps I should have someone a bit more..." His voice trailed off for a moment. "I guess sophisticated is the word I'm looking for."

"Let's try the next one then, shall we? This woman's name is Janice Betonie. She certainly looks more the part."

Melissa struggled to her feet, almost catching her heel again in the loop of the carpet. She could have sworn she felt the burn of Matthew's gaze on her rear end as she walked over to change the tape.

It made the sway of her hips feel more exaggerated than normal. Made her aware of her body in a way she never had been before. Why this should be, she didn't know. She certainly wasn't comfortable with the man. Despite that, something about him made her pulse beat faster. Made the blood rush through her veins and generated a fire she hadn't felt in a long time.

For crying out loud, the man was an undertaker of all things. How could she be turned on by someone who dealt in dead bodies?

Regardless of his job, he was as sexy as hell, even with all that grease in his hair. One thing, though, he'd have to change his chauvinistic attitudes. In this day and age no woman would put up with his comments. He was already at a disadvantage, what with his strange mannerisms and the disastrous hair oil. Although the way she felt, she'd even put up with that.

Damn, this wasn't like her at all. She was acting completely out of character. *You're the responsible one, remember, Melissa?* Yeah, goody-two-shoes as her sister would say. So what the hell was wrong with her?

Her brain had gone on vacation. Because right about now, she had one thought and one thought only in her mind. Throw Matthew Campbell down on his back and fuck the living daylights out of him.

Oh my gawd, she was in serious trouble here. She needed to get her mind off her body and onto the business of finding Matthew Campbell a partner.

Matt tried to keep his attention focused on the television screen, but he couldn't help a sneaky sideway glance at the exposed length of Melissa's legs. She'd either forgotten, or given up, trying to stretch her skirt down. One pale pink, lacy garter peeked out beneath the hemline. On the very end, in what appeared to be silky satin, was a darker pink embroidered rose.

He had a sudden urge to reach out and run his finger over it to check. It took all his self-discipline to ignore the unschooled impulse. He averted his gaze and stared at the screen.

"My name is Janice Betonie and I'm..."

The woman on the screen had a well-modulated, husky voice, but she couldn't hold his interest. Matt tuned out the sound and allowed his attention and his gaze to slide back to the woman beside him. Her skirt had risen another inch. He caught a peek of pale skin above the rose-embossed garter.

X-rated images leapt into his brain, scrambling his thought processes. Heat slammed into him, sliding through his veins and igniting a hungry need inside him. He itched to run his fingers over that strip of skin and see if it felt as soft as it looked. He wanted to taste the creamy texture, slide his tongue across the silky softness and trace the garter up her thigh until he came to her pussy.

He imagined himself down on his knees, head buried between those creamy thighs. Tongue probing at the slick folds of her sex. Then he'd spread her lips and play with her clit until she screamed and begged him to delve deep to taste her honey.

His cock tightened, all the blood driven from his brain and collecting in that wayward piece of male equipment. A raging boner pushed at the front of his trousers. He dropped his hands over his lap to hide the telltale bulge. Thank God he'd worn a suit today and not his normal skin-tight jeans. Shit, he had to stop this, but first...

He leaned closer and dragged in a deep breath. Light, floral perfume teased at his senses. Funny, given the glossy photo back at the office, he would have staked a bet she'd use a heavy musky scent. But he liked this better. Somehow, it suited her. Made a fellow think of innocence and...

Hang on a minute, man, he remonstrated with himself. *This woman is anything but innocent. She's the subject of an undercover investigation and you'd better remember that. Get your mind out of your pants and onto your work.*

As the videotape came to an end, he plastered what he hoped was an interested look on his face. He kept his gaze glued to the blank screen as if deep in thought when Melissa turned toward him.

"What do you think, Matthew? Are you interested?"

Fucked if I know. I didn't take in anything but the first sentence the woman uttered. "Hmm, it's so hard to make a decision based on a video image."

"Perhaps you should meet Janice, go out with her and see how you feel. I'm sure you'll have a great time with her and once you've had a successful date, you'll have much more confidence in your dating skills. You're a good-looking man. Any woman would be happy to be seen with you. Would you like me to ring her?"

Matt stood and stepped away from the sofa. Even from here, Melissa's perfume reached out to him and made his cock twitch in reaction. "Yes, perhaps that would be best. Meet the woman in the flesh, so to speak. Dial away, my dear lady."

Somehow he had to get Miss Morgan to take him under her wing personally, not fob him off on some other unsuspecting female. How else was he going to find out if she was a part of this blackmailing scam? Time to turn on the pathos.

One ordinary woman...two extraordinary hunks.

The Life and Loves of April Johnson
© 2006 Eve Vaughn

April Johnson is just a regular woman, taking one day at a time, who always manages to get into sticky situations.

At her high school reunion April's life changes forever when she finds herself falling for Richard Slick, nerd turned hunk. Matters are only complicated when Marcus, the man who broke her heart in high school and who's now a big time actor, makes a stunning declaration.

April lands smack in the middle of a love triangle and must decide between these two studs. Her choice leads to heartbreak, the discovery of her self-worth and learning that it just might be possible to love two men. Some lessons are worth learning.

Available now in ebook and print from Samhain Publishing.

HOT STUFF

Discover Samhain!
THE HOTTEST NEW PUBLISHER ON THE PLANET

Romance, fantasy, mystery, thriller, mainstream and
more—Samhain has more selection, hotter authors, and
everything's available in both ebook and print.

Pick your favorite, sit back, and enjoy the ride!
Hot stuff indeed.

WWW.SAMHAINPUBLISHING.COM

GREAT cheap FUN

Discover eBooks!

THE FASTEST WAY TO GET THE HOTTEST NAMES

Get your favorite authors on your favorite reader, long before they're
out in print! Ebooks from Samhain go wherever you go, and work with
whatever you carry—Palm, PDF, Mobi, and more.

Samhain
Publishing, Ltd

WWW.SAMHAINPUBLISHING.COM

Printed in the United States
98524LV00001B/238-243/A